I0569900

Book 2
CHRONICLES OF THE MARTLET

THE MORALITY OF
A NECROMANCER

Written by
Elizabeth Guizzetti

Edited by Joe Dacy
Cover and Interior Illustrations by Elizabeth Guizzetti

This is a work of fiction. Names, characters, businesses, places, events
and incidents are products of the author's imagination or used in a
fictitious manner. Any resemblance to actual persons, living or dead,
or actual events is purely coincidental. (Also weird. I mean really this
book is about a group of elves.)

Printed in the United States of America

Paperback ISBN-13: 978-0999559833

Dedicated to Ramona

Seven Populated Realms protected by the Guild

Cannik (Can nik)
Watery Realm of the vodnik

Daouail (Da o wail)
Realm of the Daosith

Dynion (Di nee on)
Realm of the humans

Fatidel (Fat i del)
Realm of the Fates

Fairhdel (Fair del)
Realm of the Fairsinge

Larcia (Lar see a)
Realm of the dwarves

Si Na (See Na)
Realm of the telchine
*Uttalassus (Ut ta lass us)
Technically within the Realm of Si Na.
Land of the gnomes

Realms not within the Guild

Risford (Rise Ford)
Realm of the Giants

Widae (Wed ae)
Realm of Dragons

Thousands of Uncharted Realms

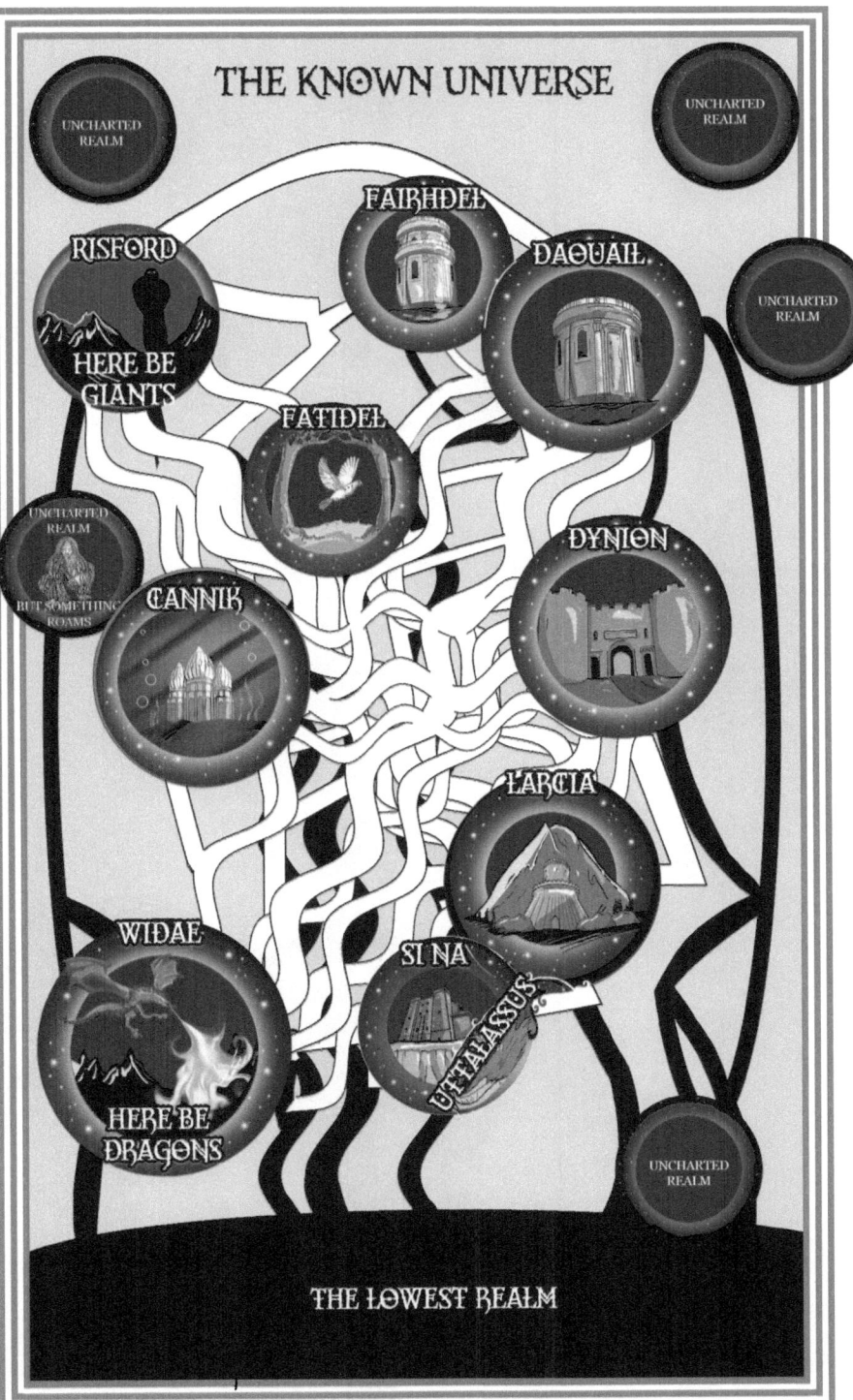

THE MORALITY OF A NECROMANCER

Chapter 1
A cottage in a wood,
somewhere in the Realm of Daouail

KIAN ONLY NEEDED A MOUTHFUL OF WINE. Just the dregs at the bottom of a carafe would stop the pounding in his head. The thick red liquid in the bottle was too salty to be wine, but the pressure on his lips echoed the memory of it.

Poison. Kian had tasted this blood and chemical mixture before: *Master Candlewick's healing potion.* His brain screamed at the betrayal, but his mouth could not form the words. He wanted to drink. If he couldn't have wine, poison would do. Anything to stop the burning memories.

Above him, three faces blurred. He was back where he started in the unending nightmare of slavery. This place was a trap. The witch, her handsome nephew and the man who claimed to be his lost brother would sell him again. He would rather die than live as a slave. He wouldn't let the witch sell him. He would kill her if he could.

The poison burned his throat and pooled into his gut. Heat rose from the center of his being and raced through his veins. Night wind whistled through the cracks in the cottage's stone walls, sweeping a deathly chill across his skin, but Kian was on fire.

He screamed until his voice grew raspy.

A cooling hand rested on Kian's brow. He observed it was small, mostly ivory with ruddy and wrinkled knuckles.

Larger hands gently smoothed blankets over him and bound him to the mattress with layers of rope across his chest. *Eohan, if you really are Han, don't sell me,* Kian wanted to cry, but darkness took him utterly. His last sensible thought was that he would like to bite his brother and taste his blood. Maybe then he would know if Eohan was real or not.

✳

ATCHING KIAN'S HEAD LOLL BACK ONTO the mattress, Eohan worked to ensure his younger brother's comfort. He slipped his fingers between the thick wool blanket and the ropes. The binding wasn't tight. It would allow Kian to easily roll over but would stop him if he tried to rise.

Eohan tucked the blanket over Kian's pronounced clavicle both for warmth, and so he didn't have to witness the birdlike fragility. Kian's scrawny chest was thinner than Eohan's thigh. Of course, Eohan was seven years older, but had he been this small at eleven? He couldn't remember. The brothers' late-mother's hazel eyes and scarred backs were the only resemblances. Eohan received his raven hair, considerable frame, and darker skin from his biological father. Though Kian was still growing, he barely brushed his brother's massive shoulder. Kian always looked like their Pa, a lanky man with strawberry-blond hair and fair complexion. Now Kian looked half-starved, in some way stunted.

Alana forced open the boy's mouth. The coating of white disappeared, and the flesh became pink. Kian's flaking lips healed. His pallor went from a sallow sickly gray to the blush of health before their eyes.

The thick creases on the lady's face relaxed into wrinkles; tears sparkled in her blue eyes as she wiped the sweat from Kian's brow.

Eohan's heart swelled with gratitude for her compassion. He couldn't have asked for a better master and friend. After the strange string of events that brought them together, Alana had taught and protected him. She treated him as she treated Roark, her own nobleborn nephew. She had searched the Realms -- and found -- his little brother who had been sold multiple times. She fed, clothed him and even gave the last of her healing potion. Eohan wanted to thank her for the sacrifices she made, but the words in his head sounded stupid, trite, and unworthy of the noblewoman. He was still figuring out what to say when Roark said, "We have a problem."

At the window, a gull squawked; a Guild mission scroll tied to its leg.

"Hopefully, it's a small one." Alana wiped her eyes on the edge of her nightdress's sleeve and went to retrieve the scroll.

"What do we do, my lady?" Eohan asked, feeling an ache in the back of his throat. "I can't leave him again."

As was the War Ender's habit, she did not look up from the parchment. "I wouldn't expect you too. Corwin wants a favor from me."

"But we did everything legally," Roark said, tossing a crust of bread to the messenger-gull. "Who is Corwin to ask for favors?"

"He's the Guild House Master of Olentir and will be for many years yet," Alana replied in her "don't be a cumberworld" voice which she saved for the rare moments when she was irritated with one of them.

Eohan winced, but Roark remained beside his aunt and studied the scroll.

"Why in the lowest Realm would Corwin care about this?" Roark asked.

"I doubt he does. I'll learn what he cares about on the job. Keep the other two safe." Alana wrote a short message on a piece of parchment, tucked it into the gull's scroll tube. The bird squawked and side-eyed the bread. Roark tossed it another morsel. The gull flipped its head toward the ceiling and swallowed, bobbed its head and flew out the window.

"Yes, Auntie, I will, but you aren't waiting till morning?"

Eohan hid the roll of his eyes. He hated when Roark called the great lady by a silly endearment -- though he only ever said it in private.

"I should leave immediately." Alana put an overtunic over her nightdress and gathered her saddlebags. "There's enough food in the safehouse for a week, but keep your snares set to extend it. Once Kian wakes, he'll need meat ... I craved meat and blood after I took the potion."

"Yes, my lady," Eohan said with a painful lump in his throat.

She stretched woolen socks over her feet and laced up her boots. "I'll return as soon as I'm able, but don't wait for me. If you aren't here, I'll meet you in Eyredeir. If Kian could travel, I'd send you now."

Alana grasped her nephew by his elbow and whispered something else. She kissed his cheek and passed him a small bag of coin. By the roundness of the bag, Eohan did a quick mental calculation -- easily enough for travel and lodgings to Eyredeir.

"Be well, Eohan, and keep your brother under a watchful eye." She hurried out to the stables.

Roark leaned against the door frame. Eohan came beside him and watched their master lead her horse into the darkness. The moonlight caught a flash of Alana's silvery braid before she disappeared into the wood.

"If I could kill him, I would," Roark said.

"What did Corwin ask?"

"You won't believe. She needs to rescue some slaves from her list and bring them to Sildeir instead of Eyredeir."

"Why?" Remembering how Corwin looked down upon him, Eohan felt a sour taste in his mouth. "Corwin doesn't care about commoners much less slaves."

Roark shrugged. "Maybe for House Silba, but I don't know. He's up to something."

"Why does Corwin hate her?"

"He doesn't. He hates she chose to stay on the job when House Eyreid was under attack." Roark's eyes shut and shook his head as if he were trying to dislodge the memory. "And he hates that if he had been in Alana's shoes, he would have made the same decision. I wish I hadn't read his mind. It was easier to loath him before."

Eohan thought it was still pretty easy to dislike the House Master but didn't say anything. "Did Lady Alana tell you anything more?"

"She just said, 'Only the potion is dangerous. Kian might struggle with the bloodlust. He's still so pale.'"

"I hoped she whispered the answer to our problems."

Roark shrugged. "Well, she told us to ensure Kian eats meat. I'll check the snares in the morning. Maybe we caught a rabbit or something."

❊

Elizabeth Guizzetti

Chapter 2
The Muirchlaimhte

ALANA LED TALIA SLOWLY EASTWARD through the darkness of the forest. Daouail's two moons cast dimmed beams, but the moss-covered ground was uneven with hidden rocks and roots. They were both a little too long in the tooth to survive a stumble.

She hoped the older boys would be able to handle Kian's needs for a few weeks, but mostly her mind was on Corwin's request: "Who knows what Corwin wants? What if our shared grief finally reached him and he softened in his old age?"

Talia neighed in response as she often did when Alana spoke to her in a conversational way.

"I did not think so either," Alana said.

For five decades, she wandered for the good of her people and glory of her House, transfixed upon the Martlet vow. Her work as a Guild War Ender had always been secondary. She had killed and wounded uncounted to save immeasurable others. During the long years, through the many Realms, Alana wandered, her time of strength had grown thin. Her body had grown bony and tired. Her heart had become so indulgent she had rescued two common slave boys without worry of the various debts she was incurring. She feared her mind grow soft before she could repay them. *Perhaps Corwin's worried about that, too.*

"It's unlikely Corwin wishes to train any of the children who were lost."

This time the mare's neigh seemed like she was laughing at the thought.

Corwin openly detested the Guild's open and equal, skill-based tradition. He wanted only the nobleborn Martlets as the elfkin representatives within the Guild and did not approve of Eohan for the War Ender ranks. *What if Corwin has a plan for them?*

"Maybe, I should've had the boys ride tonight," she said.

Fighting the terror she had made a mistake and should turn back to the safehouse, Alana picked her way through the boulders and moss until she came to a dirt road. She mounted her horse.

The well-traveled road was clear on an icy night such as this. Talia cantered all the way to Gornisce, the closest city with a long InterRealm dock. She slowed to a trot in the outer village.

Alana was briefly stopped at the city gate, but instead of announcing herself, she gave the Guild sign with the hope she would not be questioned. She wasn't. Near the gates, the streets were mostly empty, except for beggars and urchins huddled under the eaves of buildings.

Closer to the docks, the public houses kept their oil lamps burning, but it was late enough that their patrons had gone home or back to their ships. Alana stopped to scan the notices pinned to the wall under a low hanging eave. It was there. She wasn't surprised but regretted leaving the boys instead of planning their escape.

Regicide!

Reward for the capture of two runaway Fairsinge slaves who may have information of the Empress and her consort's death.

Male Arena Fighter of twenty-five, name of Roson
Black colored hair, 18 hands high and 9 hands across the shoulders.

Male of eleven, name of Kian
Straw colored hair, hazel eyes

Two Daosith women wandered past in conversation, perhaps in negotiations. They did not look up at her, but Alana moved as if she were reading another notice.

Once the two turned the corner, Alana ripped the notice off the wall, slipped it into her pouch, and set to the marina. At the end of the dock was a large wooden Expanse-faring ship, emblazoned with the word *Muirchlaimhte* in gold leaf on the port side. The forecastle, ending in a large bowsprit, was covered with gun boxes. Its rounded-off iron-clad, wooden hull held three decks leading to the aftcastle where the folded glass hull was battened down to allow the fresh briny air to permeate all the decks.

She stopped at the gangplank and asked the sailor. "Alana Guild War Ender asks permission to come aboard."

He rang two bells and, moments later, the captain's sixteen-year-old daughter, Nalla, hurried down the gangplank to help with Talia. Her long black braids flew in the icy darkness of pre-dawn. Nalla already had her mother's fine brown skin and ebony hair, and, in a few years, she would have her mother's elegance and composure. However, on that day, Nalla showed her disappointment plainly on her face as she looked past Alana though they embraced in greeting.

"Kian came to us quite ill, but I'm sure you will see Eohan soon."

Nalla turned to Talia and petted her nose and nuzzled her as was the girl's habit. "I'm glad you found Eohan's brother and sorry he is ill."

"I'll tell Eohan you asked after him; it will lighten his days. He oft thinks of you."

Nalla's bright smile returned. "Thank you, Lady Alana."

She clicked her tongue at Talia and led her up the lower gangplank to the stables in the ship's second deck.

A sailor carried her bags. At the top of the gangplank, Captain Nyauail waited.

The women embraced and kissed each other's cheeks.

"Corwin wastes no time," Nyauail whispered. "But as far as I know, he doesn't know or care I helped you with the boys."

"Good. I must send a message to Roark."

Nyauail sighed. "And you'll tell Eohan that Nalla asked about him."

"You don't approve of their infatuation?"

"I want her to be a deck boss before I'm a grandmother."

"Eohan does not entertain any other, but I keep all my apprentices equipped, less I'm wandering the Realms with a moppet in tow."

"Nalla is equipped as well, but only the lowest Realm knows if they'll use it when the moment strikes." Nyauail sighed deeply. "Still, if it comes to that, you need not worry; my grandchild would stay with me." Nyauail's white teeth flashed as the steward. Lillia, an elderly, peg-legged Daosith woman approached.

"Nalla has a good head on her shoulders, Cap," Lillia said. "Though, Lady, I don't know about that boy." The venerable woman pointed at Alana's brow. "Ever spread your gifts around?"

"I've foreseen Eohan's future, but only in regard to Roark. As for his future with Nalla, I cannot say." Alana asked Nyauail. "You want to know Nalla's future?"

"No. Nor would I believe it if you told me. The Expanse is too unpredictable. Next, you'll be telling stories of ghost ships, unicorns dancing in sea foam, and giant white whales. Your tales are worse than any sailor's."

Nyauail invited Alana for tea during the voyage and returned to work by yelling at a sailor who was trying to carry a load meant for two. Another sailor appeared in seconds.

Lillia escorted Alana down a small flight of sternward stairs into the large Guild cabin where Bryonia, the fifty-second Martlet of House Silba, reclined on one of the built-in benches attached to the stern. At twenty-three, the woman's gentle alabaster face had matured with smooth high cheekbones which looked as if they had been sculpted by the Goddess herself.

Alana felt her scalp prickle. She wished she hadn't wasted the last of the blood potion on Kian. If Byronia was half-decent with the saber on her belt, Alana could not stand against her.

The young woman rose and inclined her blond head. "Lady Alana, your reputation has come to Sildeir as our citizens return to us as refugees. Doyenne Orla sends her regards and thanks. We weren't sure you'd come, but my Lord Uncle said never to doubt you."

Alana smiled. "I'm sure Corwin said more than that."

Scarlet raced across the perfect cheeks. "Corwin still mourns over your shared loss bitterly. My uncle doesn't wish to know Ylynn keeps the flowers fresh and presents holy ash upon the crypt so her sacrifice isn't forgotten."

"That you were once my daughter's friend and speak of her is a kindness to my heart. And that you still visit House Eyreid to see Ylynn also brings me happiness." Alana studied the young woman who still made no move of aggression. "And I'm sorry for the death of your mother. Doyenne Esara was a great leader; may Doyenne Orla live long and bring your House to prosperity."

"Thank you."

"You've grown up since last I saw you. How long have you wandered?"

Bryonia crossed her arms. "I only just started. I studied under Corwin on and off since I was thirteen, but we rarely left the Guild House. Now Orla's insisting I fulfill a Martlet's duty; I'm lost. Corwin gave me leave to use Guild Resources."

Alana pressed her lips together at the fib. Byronia had always been one of Corwin's favorites, but he would not squander Guild resources if he didn't think the Guild would get something out of it. *But what would the Guild want? Is he testing Byronia or me ... or Roark and Eohan? Damn his machinations.*

She sank into one of the benches and set her journal on the built-in table.

Byronia sat across from her. "Corwin said you traveled across the Realms to find one lost boy. That Roark and your common apprentice are nursing him back to health. Why?"

Alana ignored the fact that Byronia hadn't bothered to learn Eohan's name. Or perhaps that she put out a trap. "I saw our people on the slave ship. I rescued them. Children had been sold. Kian is my apprentice, Eohan's, younger brother. He is a citizen of your principality. And he is a Fairsinge. Our people deserve better than to be ripped away from our shores and sold to the highest bidder."

"My sister agrees," the younger woman said in a monotone. "As do your sister and Ylynn."

"Do you?"

"Until now, I haven't thought about it. Orla told me, Corwin might be too old to wander, but I couldn't hide in the Guild, especially when Sildeir's villages are being attacked by InterRealm slavers." Byronia slipped her hands in her tunic pockets, removed them, crossed her arms, uncrossed them, then put her hands back into her pockets. Her deep blue eyes held fear and sadness. She was either an expert actor or telling the truth about her inexperience.

"Why are you here? The truth now—and don't bother to hide lies with truth to a mind reader. You waste time." Alana grabbed Byronia by the shoulders. Her blue eyes opened wide and her white throat fluttered as she gasped.

"Corwin said you unlocked Roark's mind, and you could train me too."

"And, why in the lowest Realm, would you desire foresight?"

"A time is coming when the gift will be needed again, even though such gifts can cause bearer pain."

"Corwin foresaw this?"

"I don't know if it was foresight or Guild information came his way. He just said 'If I journey with you, you'd teach me to use the...'"

"Curse. It's a curse and don't let Corwin tell you otherwise."

"Then why teach Roark?"

"I foresaw he'd need it." Alana released her. "I don't know if you have latent mental abilities, but I suppose we could try."

Three sharp whistles pierced the air as the ship slipped away from the dock and out to the sea.

Outside, the darkness grew into the deepest black. Alana asked, "Tell me, what does your heart call you to do?"

The darkness dissipated as *The Muirchlaimhte* dove through a blinding white halo of the veil between the Realms. Frothy clouds of every color slipped across the portholes; the Expanse sparkled. Far in the distance, the soft outline of the Realm of Dynion shined into the mist.

"I enjoyed diplomatic missions best, but, as my Lord Uncle bade me, I originally trained to be a War Ender as he once was. Unfortunately, I was a great disappointment. As he warned, diplomatic gifts are not enough to keep the peace between Realms or even provinces. I wish they were."

If her words were true, Alana felt for the young woman.

"As would I, but I have traveled too long. The Realms are filled many peoples and cultures, all with the belief that they know best. Most have at least a few repulsive laws we're forced to respect. Even our own people have edicts unworthy of our great culture. Have you seen battle?"

Byronia shook her head and wiped her hands on her tunic.

A rap at the door interrupted their conversation. Lillia entered, carrying a tub; behind her, three young sailors hauled buckets of steaming water. A fourth entered carrying a Guild crow.

Good. It would do to have time to think.

＊

Chapter 3
A cottage in a wood,
somewhere in the Realm of Daouail

ROARK MOVED ABOUT THE STABLES DOING his routine morning care for the horses. Jaci and Cloudy were both in good health and used to his and Eohan's daily handling. They acted as predictable as any horse might be under the circumstances, seemingly unconcerned in the safehouse's stable, happy for affection and food.

As Alana instructed, he kept his accursed mind on Kian's innermost thoughts and desires. Outwardly, like any other eleven-year-old boy would, Kian had climbed to the highest branches of the tree in front of the cottage to get the choicest apples. Inwardly, he lusted for the taste of wine and blood.

Roark wished he did not have to listen to the younger boy's thoughts. Kian also feared Eohan and Roark. He expected they might turn violent towards him. He suspected it was the Wounded's Melancholy. Roark had seen the disorder in the Guild Infirmary from time to time. Kian had been sold three times and had seen his fair share of villainy. His back would always bear the scars. He might be unable to become the beloved —though at times annoying little brother—Eohan once knew and expected to know again.

If Kian lost control and attacked him, Eohan or the horses, Roark would have to deal with him in a non-lethal and least damaging way possible. Roark wished he knew exactly how he would do that. He needed a plan.

Roark yearned to return to Port Dentwort to interrogate Edar Candlewick, who crafted Alana's bloodpotion, but he couldn't go back to the lich with Kian in tow. *If I left them for a week, I could easily make it.* But he knew he would not leave them behind. It was time to prove to Alana he was ready to progress and to start his own journey. He needed to prove it to himself too. His apprenticeship was coming to an end, but at this moment, with a boy lusting after blood, Roark was lost without his mentor.

A Guild crow landed on the stable gate and cawed. Roark gave it a bit of the apple. Alana scrawled on a Bounty notice:

Get out of Daouail as soon as you can. I saw this in Gornisce; I leave their safety in your capable hands. The good news is they overestimated Eohan's age. Perhaps you could use that to your advantage.

--Love Auntie

PS Tell Eohan Nalla asked after him and sends prayers for Kian's recovery.

Roark reread the letter twice. He wished he had her confidence in his skills. He needed to come up with a plan.

✻

KIAN CLIMBED DOWN FROM THE TREE. HIS feet squished through the uneven, mossy ground. Sunbeams filtered through the thick canopy and fell in brilliant rays down to the ground turning it into an impossibly bright shade of green. Trees pressed in on him. Birds sang in the morning sun, but every chirp and tweet brought Kian's terror higher into his chest until he thought he might scream. He didn't know who he was. A kitchen slave? A necromancer's toy? A butcher and baker's son?

As terrifying as the forest, being inside the cottage seemed worse.

"Kian," a voice called from behind him.

He spun around.

Eohan stood there, wiping his massive hands on a linen towel. "I said breakfast is ready. And thank you for getting the apples."

Eohan took the fruit from him and brought it inside. Moments later, Kian could hear a knife slicing through the fruit and hitting the block. *Maybe he's not Han. If he 's not, what's wrong with enjoying his blood?*

Kian pushed the thought away. The smith who fathered Eohan was a larger, more muscular man than the lanky baker who fathered Kian. The smith's complexion had been darker, and his hair was black and glossy like the Eohan who stood before him. Kian's own hair was not quite red, not quite blond just like Pa's.

Afraid to go inside and discover if Eohan's eyes were still hazel, Kian watched the horses trot out of the stable to graze in the distance. One of them might carry him away. Or maybe their flesh would be sweet.

Kian jerked away as Roark set a hand on his shoulder. He fell to his knees and covered his head.

"I didn't mean to scare you."

Kian peeked up through his fingers. The nobleborn did not strike or kick him. The dirty linen tunic raised as Roark sighed, but he held out his hand and helped Kian to his feet. The boy felt bewitched by the impeccable ivory contours of the young nobleman's face. Roark appeared to be everything a nobleborn should be. His auburn hair curled at the base of his smooth neck, even in a state of half-dress, he appeared put together, but Kian didn't trust the beautiful exterior.

"Please, don't keep your brother waiting. Lady Alana won't like being ignored when she returns. Tell Eohan I'll be in as soon as I clean up."

Looking up into the handsome clear blue eyes, Roark's delicate but unwavering features etched an image in Kian's mind. He remembered one of the silk tapestries woven by the gentlest of his former masters: a seraph guarding the Waters of Resurrection.

"I didn't hear. Sorry," he lied and went inside.

✻

"YOU NEED TO EAT SOMETHING," EOHAN said. He speared his fork into another bite of meat, wishing his brother would take his example of proper behavior without urging. If they were to leave the station of their birth, they needed the nobleborn's mannerisms.

Kian stared at the large rabbit haunch in front of him. His crumpled posture leaned over his plate. His right hand holding the empty fork, his left rubbed his right wrist repeatedly.

"Han, what are we doing?" Kian asked instead of eating.

"Eating breakfast." Eohan speared another piece of rabbit with his fork. *He's still ill,* Eohan reminded himself. *Do not lose your temper no matter what. A War Ender would never lose his temper -- especially at his sick brother.* To calm himself, he thought of Nalla. Even though they only had a few hours with each other when fate brought them together, he had never felt such a connection. He cherished the memory of their first kisses and walk along the beach. If Nalla had asked Alana about him, she must feel the same way about him as he felt about her.

"No, what are we doing here? With Roark?"

"I'm training to be a Guild War Ender. Roark's Alana's nephew and other apprentice. Did you forget in your sickness?" Feigning concern, he pressed a hand to Kian's forehead. It was hot and clammy to touch. Feigned concern became true alarm. "Maybe you should return to bed if you're too sick to eat."

Kian dropped his fork onto the crock which splattered sauce on the table. "I need some air." He stepped to the window and pushed it open wide. The younger boy started to gasp and wheeze. He held his stomach and sank to the floor.

Ignoring the spilled sauce, Eohan rose and scratched the stubble on his chin. "Does your stomach hurt?"

"I remember some things, but I still feel ... confused. Where's Ma?"

"Ma died on the slave ship. Her body was lost at sea."

"And Pa?"

"I don't know. I never saw him on the ship ... or Smith. Only a few other men from our village were in my cell; mostly I saw dwarves. I never saw the lower decks until Lady Alana freed everyone. I only saw the people in my lifeboat. I was so lost, everything that night is a blur."

"Pa might still be home," Kian said.

"He might, or he might've escaped to another village. We don't know," Eohan said.

"Maybe, we could find him."

"You don't want to be in the Guild? Because you must be sure. It's dangerous work ..."

"You're not listening!" Kian punched the stone wall leaving no mark on the stone but bloodying his knuckles. He drew his knees to his chest, squeezed his eyes shut and started rocking back and forth.

Immediately, Roark rushed towards them with a length of coarse rope in his hand. Eohan put his arm out to stop him from touching Kian.

Though Eohan was two years older, Roark was the more senior apprentice and a nobleborn. He treated Eohan as his equal and friend, but, in that moment, Roark's expression changed to the future striking visage of Lord Roark, the future Martlet of House Erydeir, as he countered the reach. "Don't."

Though it pained him to do so, Eohan dropped his arm to his side.

Roark knelt beside Kian.

"If you think you're strong enough to travel, perhaps, we could go to your village and meet Alana in Eyrdeir after."

Tears of relief flooded Kian's eyes as he looked up at them. "In truth?"

"If we go, we need to be careful. We don't know who might be looking for the Empress's killer," Roark said, relaxing his grip on the rope. "We know they're looking for a man and a boy. I'll need to think on our traveling gear."

Still scratching the stubble on his chin, Eohan said, "What would Lady Alana say ... ?"

Rising to his feet, Roark's voice rose to a falsetto. "I teach you only what is important; the rest you must learn for yourself." In his own voice, he said, "She told us to take care of Kian. If we don't go to your father, he can't make an informed decision about his future. If the ship docks in Olentir, it's a short detour."

Roark returned to the table and set the rope behind him. Picking up his blade and fork, he cut a piece of rabbit and swirled the meat through the broth before taking another bite.

Kian wiped the tears away and took another shaky breath. "Is it true, the nobleborn read minds?"

"Not all, but these two can. Our lady is particularly adept. She sees the future, too. She saw us in Roark's future. That's why she saved us."

Roark took another bite of rabbit before he spoke his thoughts aloud. "Maybe we could wear the priest's veil. The novice is covered from head to toe. Or perhaps in Guild tunics is best, but we need clothing for Kian that actually fits if we are to pull off. Maybe it'd be best to blacken Kian's hair ... Why are you two still standing there?"

Kian whispered, "Wait. Is it true Martlets make you dance on coals if you betray them?"

Eohan rested his hand on Kian's shoulder. "Don't know, I never thought to betray them. Eat a little. You need strength."

Sniffing, Kian joined Roark at the table and took a bite of the rabbit.

※

Corwin,

Why must we play these games?
Just tell me what you actually want. You
must want more than the training of Byronia.
I'd have done that if you'd have only asked.

-Alana

Chapter 4
Port Dentwort in the Realm of Dynion

ALANA'S CROW FLEW WITH THE MISSIVE TO the Guild House as she and Byronia disembarked the *Muirchlamhte* and walked up the long docks to town. The sea wind could not remove the stench of an InterRealm slave ship moored there. Rain fell in heavy drops on the wooden decking, washing the stains of blood and filth into the water. By its marking, the ship was of dwarven make. The crew seemed mostly to be dwarves and humans. Each small group of doomed souls looked to be primarily dwarves. Though it pained her, Alana turned toward the square where bodies of all intelligent species crammed between market day caravan and tents for all kinds of buying and selling.

She and Byronia were jostled as they moved through the thick crowd. Some traded; more watched the spectacle, hooting at the biggest men or prettiest women. Near the holding pen, a group of boys took turns prodding the dwarves who had the misfortune to be closest to the fence. They hit one man in the rump; his chains did not allow him to push them away.

The slave block was full this time. Still, no elfkin were on the block. Only humans and dwarves. The well-dressed auctioneer flung his filthy trade onto the crowd.

Though his business was dirty, the auctioneer's silver tongue matched the silver medallion around his neck. His deep green linen breeches and coat and fine white underlinens were unblemished by the grime around him. Even his shoes shined. She might be able to tempt him with greed.

Exhausted by the injustices in the Realms, Alana's temples throbbed. "If I could trade my soul to see this atrocity wiped from the Realms, I would," she said softly.

Byronia did not answer, but she squeezed her hand.

Alana studied the other auction workers. A less distinguishably dressed man acted as recordkeeper by logging sales and handling the coin passed to him. His narrow, well-practiced fingers counted quickly, and he bowed toward each of the buyers as he made their change, took their addresses, and handed off each slave. Surrounding them, several large, gruff-looking human men held willow canes, ready to strike if a slave didn't do as he, she, or sie were told.

Alana's despair intensified. So many slaves went through the market, there was no way the auctioneer could remember a day nearly ten months ago.

Someone knocked into her back. She staggered forward and bumped into someone else who turned around with a harsh, "Watch it." However, the human man saw her face and said, in a much kinder tone, "Keep your footing there, Mother. Wild crowd today. Wild crowd. Your mother needs help, girl."

Byronia thanked him for his concern and apologized for any inconvenience.

The human was correct. The crowd had a life of its own. The chatter between friends. Merchants, some respectable, some not, selling their wares. Individuals struggling to hear the auctioneer, who shouted descriptions so fast Alana could hardly understand his words.

Finally, the auction was over. Many in the crowd lingered in nearby stalls; others wandered home or to a pub.

Alana approached the auctioneer. "Excuse me ..."

"You missed the auction."

"I was hoping to see your records."

"Get lost."

"Some of our children were sold." She opened her hand and exposed a gold coin of the Realm. "Hundred?"

He snorted in disdain. "Your either foolish or ..." He frowned. For all his quick words in the square, his vocabulary seemed to fail him as he stared at the coin. "No. You're foolish if you expect me to put myself in danger to help a couple of elves."

He pushed his way past Alana and walked with long strides away from the square. However, the recordkeeper didn't remove his eyes from the coin in her hand.

"We got another ship coming in tomorrow ... long day," he said turning the direction in which the auctioneer did not go.

"But you would be willing to allow us to view your records?"

"A hundred might not keep me if I'm caught ... I have a family to think of."

"One-fifty?" Alana asked. "We want to see your records. Show us the books, and we'll help ourselves."

"Two hundred and I didn't help you inside," he said.

"Of course not."

Alana and Byronia followed him down the street. He glanced behind them as he unlocked the door and rushed them into the dim room.

Ledgers marked with dates of the past fifty years rose towards the ceiling. The older years were covered in dust; the newer ones were cleaner. Alana spotted a set of playing cards tucked between the volumes.

"The sales were on May 12, 5890."

"Let me see the gold first."

Alana showed the man the two hundred sovereigns.

The recordkeeper grabbed the second book marked 5890 and opened it to May 12th as requested.

Alana's fingers trembling, she opened her journal and dipped her pen into the inkwell.

The recordkeeper left her side to file the daily sales this year's journal and wandered towards the back of the chamber. Perhaps to a safe or office in the back.

She scribbled down information on the missing children as fast as she could and turned the page. More names, more species of intelligent life condemned to a life of servitude. She collected names, ages, and the person who bought them from anyone marked with Light Elf or Dark Elf. These people didn't know or care about the nationalities of their species. *What was wrong with people! These are supposed to be our allies.*

Alana kept writing.

"Get a move on," the recordkeeper said.

Alana blotted her pages and carefully tied her journal. She knew there were other names in other pages, other books. She could not save them.

Whispering and heavy footsteps filled the chamber. Beside her, Byronia said, "What's going on?"

"They think we're easy targets. There's no room in here to swing a sword. We'll need to improvise."

The recordkeeper and two of the gruff-looking men whom Alana had seen at the auction stood in front of the door.

Dynion men often overlook women, especially elderly women. An advantage. As she expected, the men advanced towards, Byronia whom they assumed to be the greater threat and a greater prize.

"Don't damage the merchandise," the recordkeeper ordered.

The first assailant pulled a short cudgel from his belt and swung it towards the young woman. She screamed as she jumped backward into a bookcase. She threw the first volume she grabbed into the man's face. He grunted as the book hit him. She seized another ledger.

To get the recordkeeper out of the way, Alana elbowed him in the ribs. She stomped on his foot and kicked him in the stomach. He crumpled to the floor.

The second opponent swung his willow cane. Shrieking, Byronia blocked the blow with the book in her hands.

Alana jumped and smashed an elbow into the man's head as he readied his next blow. He wobbled, tried to put his weight on the cane and collapsed.

The wielder of the cudgel turned towards Alana. His expression showed he understood their miscalculation. He swung towards her head. She allowed herself to fall before the weapon hit her, forcing him to stretch further as she landed on her back. In his imbalance, she kicked him in the groin. He fell to his knees.

She dragged her dagger's blade into his thigh, seeking the artery. Blood sprayed across her face as she yanked it out.

Alana scrambled to her feet, slipping on the spilled blood, but regained her footing as she grabbed the dropped cudgel and smashed the second opponent, who was still prone. The sickening crack of his skull echoed across the room. He wouldn't rise again.

"What about him?" Byronia asked, still holding the book as a weapon.

The recordkeeper rolled on the floor, his hands over his face, blood running through his fingers.

Stomping on his stomach, Alana yanked his hair to force him to meet her eyes.

"Do you wish to survive this night?"

A guttural, incoherent sound came from his mouth as she ripped open his tunic, found his purse and pulled out the coin she had given him.

He howled.

"Hmm ... the loss of funds upset you? Well, it's my payment for getting rid of your unruly employees."

His mouth opened in a scarlet "O." Byronia's eyes widened.

Explaining to them both, but keeping her focus on the recordkeeper, she snapped, "You heard me. If you try to stop us or report us, I'll report you for hiring the Guild."

He shook his head.

"Why might there be a row between your men? Cards, love, old debt?"

The recordkeeper shrugged. "I didn't know them; I only used them." Alana grasped the hair on the top of his head and gave him a shake.

"Don't kill me!"

"Cards it is," she said. "I bid you run along home, hide any bruises I gave you, and find the bodies in the morning if you value your life and liberty."

The recordkeeper ran away.

Alana grabbed the cards she had seen between volumes and spilled them over the bodies. Alana took a dagger from the first man's belt and put it into the open wound on the second opponent's leg. Though there was some blood on the cudgel, she spread on a bit more.

"Why?" Byronia asked.

"From what I saw at the auction, his goons were just muscle, but a man of his stature will be missed. He believes himself to be of the gentry. I'm not sure this is the right thing, but we do what we must."

Images of what could have been flashed in Alana's mind. Still, Byronia had kept her head in her first battle. And she was keeping it together now. Corwin would be proud ... unless the young woman lied to her about her experience. By her face, Alana doubted it. Once they were safe, Alana would tell her she did well.

Alana locked the door from the inside and climbed out a window which she carefully closed behind them.

"This way."

"We're not going back to the docks?"

"No."

The two women crept to the stone cottage on the hill. Chamomile buds trembled on the windowsills concealing what lay inside the curtains. Alana knocked on the heavy red door.

The Lich peeked out.

"Hello, Mister Candlewick," she said.

"What can a humble apothecary offer a bloodied elf knight on this night?" His eyes flickered away from her face, and on to the blood that stained it A gruesome smile spread across his stained teeth, and he licked his upper lip. Though his pallor was gray, he kept his eyes lined with charcoal, and, as always, the Lich was dressed in a fine silk robe, though this time it was green. Alana hoped he only traded potions for it.

"We're in need of sanctuary, and I, unfortunately, can't walk about looking like this."

"And who is this?"

"Lady Byronia, a friend of my daughter's. You can trust her as much as you can trust me."

"I won't stand against the law."

"I don't ask you to."

Edar opened his door and motioned for them to enter. "What brings you to Port Dentwort, ladies?"

Edar ran his tongue over his lips as his eyes lingered on Byronia's carotid artery. Yet he made no move towards her. Instead, he put a kettle on the stove.

"Slavery controls the souls of our peoples. I must end it."

A shadow of wretchedness drifted onto Edar's face, but it disappeared quickly. "Slavery is condoned by the Guild, War Ender. However, my potions are not. And if the Great War Ender and Knight Errant Lady Alana of House Eyreid often come to my door? Well, as much as I enjoyed our previous conversation, your presence puts my work in jeopardy."

"I offer this blood I'm awashed in as payment and perhaps more," Alana said.

"Then take a seat by the fire." Edar poured clear water into a basin and brought it to her.

She slashed her face into the water, scraping her flesh with her nails, and let her hair drip until the water turned the color of rust. He opened a cabinet and pulled out a linen sheet and gave it to her. "Enjoy your potion?"

"It worked marvelously for healing," Alana said.

"Yes. Its potency is dependent upon the donor. You were a fine donor; how I yearn for elfkin's blood again."

Byronia's trembling hand slipped to her scabbard, but she did not arm herself.

"Unfortunately, the blood I'm awashed in is, but a human's. And I can't vouch for its quality," Alana undressed and dipped her tunic in the water, wringing it out until it was clean.

"Ah, the pity ..." Edar took her tunic and hung it near the fire.

"I'd say he was a young man, perhaps thirty summers at most."

"In death, he serves. Did you ever find Kian?"

"Yes. He's in poor health, so I gave him the last sip of my potion. He's under Roark's protection."

"Your heart does you credit. Give me another bit

of blood, and I could make each of us a potion again, but take care, or you might eventually become as I am."

She salivated at the temptation to taste the potion again and know the strength in her sword arm. "I'd be a lich?"

"I have no idea what an elfkin would become. I only know I can no longer seek the Waters of Resurrection."

"Can the mayor?"

"Certainly, he does not give soul away. He only sips my remedies."

"What is different from the potion you made me and the one you make the mayor?"

"Dilution and his ignorance, all he wants is the appearance of youth and all he needs is a mild decongestant for his lungs."

Byronia circled the kitchen. She glanced over at Alana, biting on her lower lip.

Alana rested her hand on her journal. "I need names. Not youth and I'm offering my blood ..."

"Lady Alana, you can't!"

Alana glared at Byronia. The younger lady shut her mouth and glanced towards the fire. The kettle blew. Edar poured boiling water over a pot of herbs. He held out a cup to Byronia. "Have a cup, dear lady, before you fall off your feet." He patted a bench. "It's only chamomile."

The younger lady circled the kitchen, eventually perched on the bench, but did not relax as she took the cup. She watched Alana for direction and only drank after Alana took a sip.

"My blood, if you look a map and tell me where a few houses lie."

Edar's mouth opened wide, exposing his yellow teeth again. "Another sip of your sweet blood is worth remembering a few addresses."

❄

Chapter 5
Wilds of Daouail

THE WIND BLEW THROUGH THE OVERSIZED woolens which Alana had left for Kian. Shivering, he tucked his hands into the too-long sleeves and leaned against his brother's back. He closed his burning eyes and tried to push away his fear. His mind spun with the possibilities of what might happen on the road. Perhaps when they found Pa, he would feel safe again. His scalp still tingled from the black hair dye and curling solution, but by his reflection in Roark's mirror, he looked a lot more like his brother.

Roark claimed his family would welcome him. Kian doubted that to be true. He had not even been a citizen of their province. Lady Alana had been somewhat kind, though strict, but she had disappeared. Lady Alana was strange and unpredictable as Papa had said the nobility were. How would Roark's mother and father welcome him? Or Roark's sister? Or his youngest brother, still at home but destined to marry into another great House. Kian was a runaway slave. He wiped away a tear. He tried to push away the memories of his life as a slave, but they penetrated him. They clung to his soul like grease and soot clung to the stones over a stove.

Kian leaned closer to his brother as they passed

a caravan of wagons. He shivered as the sound of a child crying from somewhere within washed over him. A woman's voice comforted the child whose whines eventually were muffled. He remembered the stuffy interior where he and Madame Grunkit spent their days as Merchant Grunkit drove with Bob, a sideman, kept watch for brigands. Comparatively, she had been a good master. She expected him to keep the wagon clean and cook their meals, but she never took his blood as Edar Candlewick did. Or hurt him in the various ways Lord Joesel had devised in his fine carriage.

No, no, no, don't think of Lord Joesel. Kian learned early to hide within himself, and the boy used that same skill to shove his fear deep into his soul and suppressed his sobs so not to cry in front of Eohan and Roark.

They couldn't understand. Eohan wasn't a broken slave; he wasn't even the son of a butcher any longer. He rode a horse. He wielded a claymore. He read the scrawls on paper. *My brother is acquainted with the nobleborn. They're friends.* Kian was only an object of pity to a young lord. He couldn't ever be a fighter as they were.

He pressed his cheek into his brother's back. Eohan's fitted doublet was made of fine wool dyed black, his undershirt white fine linen with green embroidery. Kian didn't even fit into Roark's old clothes Lady Alana had given him. He stifled the sob from rising up his throat by thinking of Madame Grunkit's soft voice.

Roark raised his hand and pointed to a shallow creek in the distance. The horses crossed the expanse within minutes. Roark and Eohan dismounted and began making camp. With quick, sure actions, the two men moved with the grace of warriors even as they made camp. He was not one of them.

As instructed, Kian filled the cooking pot with water from the stream and set it on the tripod. He cut the carrots from Roark's bag. The boy jumped as a twig snapped behind him, but it was Eohan gathering wood.

"You'll make yourself sick with your worries," Roark said. "We'll get you a new tunic, and no one will look twice at us. Don't worry. Your brother and I'll take care of you."

Kian chopped the next carrot.

"And we'll get out of Daouail."

Kian felt the heat of tears behind his eyes, but he refused to cry in front of Roark.

"Favors came due," Roark said. The edge in his voice was unmistakable.

My thoughts are making him angry. Don't think. Don't think!

Kian stopped chopping but kept his eyes on the carrot. "You sure? Because I was thinking bad thoughts about her and she left."

"Favors came due," Roark repeated and tore the last of the salted rabbit and threw it into the pot. "Everything is fine. I'm not angry at your thoughts."

"I called her a witch in my mind!"

"Much to my shame, I've called her worse to her face. Eohan is the only perfect apprentice," Roark said.

"And I too have made mistakes," Eohan said. "Lady Alana has reasons for everything she does. That she left only meant that she felt it was a greater danger to us if she stayed."

Roark nodded in agreement with this statement. "You still look pale. We have a time; rest yourself."

The carrot blurred. Fearing he might start bawling in front of the other apprentices, he pinched back tears and swallowed the lump in his throat.

Roark put a gentle hand on Kian's shoulder. He pointed at a nearby spruce. "Eohan told me you and he used to do knife tricks behind the butchery. Can you hit that tree?"

"I don't know ..."

"Try it." Roark pulled out a sharp, two-sided dagger from his belt and held it to Kian.

"Shouldn't I finish this?"

"I'll finish it for you."

Figuring that obedience was his shield, he set the carrot and kitchen blade aside and took Roark's dagger.

He had never held a knife of such balance and beauty; it felt good in his hand. Kian stood up straight and shifted his weight from to his back leg. He swung his forearm forward from the elbow and released the knife. It spun once and landed on the ground about ten paces in front of him.

"I'm not sure anybody can throw that far." Kian went to get the knife.

"I can do it blindfolded," Roark said.

"Really?"

"Our lady can also accomplish this feat; it'll be something she will teach you," Eohan said, carefully adding wood to the fire and stacking a few pieces beside it.

"Can you do it?" Kian asked.

"Not yet. I can hit the distance, but blindfolded, no."

"May I show you?" Roark said.

"Yes!"

Roark pulled a handkerchief from his pouch and handed it to Eohan.

Eohan wrapped it around Roark's eyes and waved his hand in front of the other apprentice's face. "Can you see?"

Roark shook his head. Eohan took a step back, and Kian stood beside him.

Roark cocked his head like he was listening to the wind. Holding the dagger by the blade, Roark straightened his back. He shifted his weight from to his left leg to his right. He swung his forearm forward from the elbow and released the knife. It whistled through the air and struck the side of the tree, the blade sticking into the bark.

"Excellent there!" Kian clapped his hands.

Roark removed the handkerchief. "I've been training with Alana since I was your age. It took me several months to learn. She is a better teacher than I, I'm afraid, but you could still practice knife throwing if you wish."

✳

EOHAN FIDDLED WITH THE BUTTON ON HIS sleeve and watched the pot bubble. The carrots would cook without his supervision, but Eohan felt so out of control at least he could stir the carrots.

Kian tossed Roark's knife. As it had every time before, it thudded on the ground ten paces in front of him. His aim wasn't even close, though he was hitting about the same spot each time. That was something. The little brother who used to sing with their mother was not in that boy running after the knife he just tossed. Kian used to be happy, now he feared everyone -- even Eohan.

"Don't worry, we'll figure out a way." Roark opened the oiled vellum map which he placed on a tarp.

"Are you saying that for me or you?"

Roark's smile betrayed his uncertainty. "Both of us. I'm trying to think like Alana, but I can't see that many moves and counters."

"Same."

"Which is why I brought over the map."

"It's sarding annoying when you read my mind."

"I didn't. You were staring at the carrots as if you expected them to disappear on us."

As the two apprentices had spent every day together for nearly a year, Roark, who was outstanding at reading tells, was exceptionally good at reading his. It was still annoying.

Speaking in a soft voice, Roark pointed to the nearest large port city. "We could make it easily to Gornisce, as they will have some civilian transports, except if they even think we did the regicide, they'll kill us and sell the bodies on a whim. We'd have to be on our guard and ready to fight. If I was a bounty hunter, I'd be watching the posts."

Eohan nodded. "And, even with dyed hair, Kian gives us away."

Roark ran his finger over the map until he reached the nearest Guild House which sat atop a mountain overlooking a large port. "Laithmor is only a two days ride with only one village to pass through. If Kian can act the part of a young nobleborn or at least merchantborn, we'd more easily blend in with Guild members, and the ships will be nicer if we can board a Guild transport."

"Manners are more easily taught than horsemanship and fighting."

"Agreed," Roark said.

Eohan gestured at Kian running towards the knife still not coming close to the target. "Thanks for that."

Roark shrugged. "I only thought of what might please my own little brother. I've oft wished I was a close to my brothers and sister as you and Kian are."

"Were close. Now he barely looks at me."

"Alright. Were, but will be again. Alana has foreseen it." Roark waved his fingers towards Eohan as if he were a busker casting a magic show.

"Cumberworld," Eohan said.

✳

Chapter 6
Port Dentwort in the Realm of Dynion

DAWN SENT SHIMMERING GOLDEN RAYS over the sea which lapped against the dock and hulls of the ships. Alana let the sun sink into her skin and imaged the guilt from last night's killing drift away into the expanse of water. Byronia tilted her head and pursed her lips a few times as if she wanted to speak, and though Alana expected questions, none were forthcoming.

They passed several sailors on guard at the base of each gangplank. As they arrived back at the Muirchlaimhte, a sailor inclined his head. "War Ender, I'll call Lillia for your needs. There is a missive from House Master Corwin."

"I might need to respond to this, Do you mind asking Lilla to come in two hours?"

"As you wish." He inclined his head in the usual way.

They thanked him and went aboard. The Guild cabin seemed smaller under Byronia's frightened gaze. "What did he say?"

Alana read aloud:

I need not explain my reasons. I allow you to complete an errand of little magnitude only because it is safe enough for them to learn. She is your future and mine. Roark is no consequence to me, but I shall do my duty by him unless you refuse your duty by me. -- Corwin

Alana warmed her wrinkled hands before the oil lamps small flame. Then opened her inkwell and scrawled.

How dare you threaten my nephew...

"Please!" Byronia rushed forward and knocked her knee on the wooden bench as she reached for the quill. "Please, my lady, don't anger my uncle."

Alana turned to the young woman who was still holding her knee. She did not expect an answer of consequence until she saw Byronia's eyes wide with panic.

"Don't write that or I'll tell him what you do. Creating potions to live beyond one's lifespan is not approved Guild technology! Does my uncle know you are acquainted with a lich?"

"Probably. Corwin knows many things that I don't tell him," Alana said.

"I might report you. Why should I betray my uncle for a lich?" Byronia asked, tears sparkling in her eyes. "Why should I not tell him what you do?" A red flush crossed Byronia's ivory cheeks.

"Edar gave us sanctuary last night. He didn't have to help us."

"He only helped us for your blood," Byronia sobbed.

Alana tenderly squeezed the younger woman's hand. "He only took what I offered. You were perfectly safe. Think on it. If you report Edar to your uncle, he must report it to the Guild, and we lose a safehouse. Be sure what you do."

"No!" Byronia shrieked and jerked her hand away. "Please for Roark's sake and mine. My uncle is driven to stop what's coming, he sees it! Please don't write that letter. I'll do whatever you say."

Alana snapped the inkwell shut and set the pen in its holder. "Enough of this. Sit and calm yourself, girl. And tell the truth you ought to have told days ago."

Not meeting Alana's eyes, Byronia sat. "After my mother's funeral, but before Orla's coronation, Corwin took my sisters, brother-in-law, brother and I aside and said we must fulfill our traditional roles or House Silba will fall in a generation."

"Did he say how?"

"A war." Without pausing to think, Byronia went on, her eyes still wide. "We never took his grumbling seriously. Not even when he was my master. And we didn't take him seriously on that day either Corwin said, 'he couldn't make that fool, Esara, listen, but if we don't obey his edicts, he'll destroy House Silba before he watched it tumble into ruin due to five slovenly children.'"

Trying to calm the young woman, Alana cupped her cheek and wiped a tear away. "Surely, it's not that bad. He always claimed you were his favorite and spoke of you with pride—especially your gift of language."

"But it was that bad, Aldran told him to shut up and he slapped the boy hard enough to leave a mark. You wouldn't believe an old man could..."

"What?"

"Move that fast. My siblings looked at me to protect them. He disarmed me in seconds and threw my saber across the room. Then he backed Niall against the table and said he'd find Orla a husband who could do his duty by her instead of a popinjay from the east squandering House Silba's wealth just because he fathered one child, when his job was to protect it.

"He grabbed me by the neck and said if I disobeyed him in the slightest measure, he would crucify me on the gate of House Silba. Since Aldran would now be third, he could be Martlet or join me on the gates. Orla begged him to stop and asked what we did to anger him so.

"He shouted about missing citizens and our ignorance for not even knowing our coastal villages have been attacked. I was young and not in great demand at the Guild so I had no excuse not to be on the road. He told Orla that it was her duty to protect these people. I failed them, but so had she.

"It was the most sober coronation, I've ever attended. What I said about Orla and I traveling to Eyredeir was true. We learned all I could from Ylynn and brought Orla home. I reported to Corwin and asked for advice. He said you were on a short job, but he'd ask you to help me and if I valued my life, he better not hear a complaint against my behavior. He ordered me to practice with the sentries until you were free. He told Lord Seweryn to scar my face if I fought under my abilities, so no one would recognize me as his niece." She shuddered.

Alana didn't bother to tell the young woman she had seen Corwin at his worse and a War Ender—even a former War Ender--would only do what's necessary. He hadn't attacked Byronia, she attacked him and he disarmed her. He should have had their respect, and when that didn't work, he used terror. Alana didn't always agree with Corwin's methods, and felt that if he had been a little more generous to the girl when she was a girl, he wouldn't be dealing with a young woman's rebellion.

Alana sighed and guided the troubled head to rest on her shoulder. "I won't send a response in anger. However, you ought to have told me about the coming war. Tell me about what Corwin said about that."

"But he didn't."

"Anything would help."

"Only we need to protect our citizenry when it comes. House Silba was once the defender of all Fairdhel and we must be again. Illness will spread first, followed by famine. He ordered Orla to not spend another speck on fancy tunics for Niall, but hire a weapons master. All of them are to train. As am I."

"Then it's time for your lesson. Lie down."

"You still trust me? You'll still teach me?"

"You're a Martlet. And you're not the first young person who took a respite after her apprenticeship was over. Go."

Byronia lay on in her bunk and closed her eyes.

Alana sat beside her head. and stroked her brow gently. "Now, dear one, clear your mind of worries. Just think of a pleasant future. Imagine yourself leaving your body and witnessing five years from now. Nothing to fear, I'll be beside you."

Byronia's spirit easily left her body, though her spirit hovered above the living corpse pressing upon the haze of time. Alana left her own form and broke through the mist.

For a single instant, they were in a well-appointed apartment where the future vision of Byronia spoke softly to Roark who studied his cuticles and nodded.

They returned to the Muirchlaimhte before Alana could understand what they were speaking about. Byronia opened her eyes and immediately covered them with her hands. She rolled over to her side and clenched her stomach.

Alana rubbed the base of the younger woman's neck. "You'll be alright, nausea's common until you learn to control it. You did better than Roark, his first time. Get some rest. We've slaves to save this afternoon."

"But what does it mean? I could barely hear

them—us."

"The only thing we know is you and Roark are still alive in five years, but we will journey to this time again and try longer next time."

Alana went back to the table and opened her journal to a well-worn page: the coded list of enslaved children she found when she rescued her eldest apprentice. She had opened it many times. The first saved was Kian. She looked at the names she had written and the farms, brothels, and other households Edar had shown her on the map.

From the bunk, Byronia whispered, "There are so many. Names, I mean."

"And these are only the citizens of Fairdhel and Daouail on three pages in one book. You saw the stacks."

"It's terrible, its worse than terrible, but I don't see what I can do about it."

Alana ensured her tone was gentle though her meaning was not. "You are a Martlet. With training, you could board any ship holding our people and free them."

The young woman tilted her head from side to side, never meeting Alana's eyes. "Even though Guild law allows for slavery? Isn't it futile?"

Alana leaned back and hooked her arm through the back of the bench. "Yes, it is. But it all is. Eating bread is futile, because you will just be hungry tomorrow. The Martlets wander for the good of our people; we chase ruin, but there is always ruin. You are here to learn, I am here to teach you. That's all that matters."

"Uncle's right."

"In what way, dear?"

"Someday you'll anger the wrong person. They will hunt you down and kill you."

"I never expected to die in my bed, but I face the Waters of Resurrection with only one regret."

"You're mad. And by the time this is over, I think

44

I shall be mad as well."

A sigh of contentment left Alana's lips. The young woman was learning.

❋

HIDDEN AMONG THE FRUIT-LADEN brambles with Byronia, Alana focused on the slaves' slow, methodical movements as they harvested berries. Their backs hunched from work. Three overseers rode between the lanes on what looked like mechanical bulls. On their belts, each overseer wore a knife and a modified lash of thick rope with one end unbraided. They were otherwise unarmed. The massive armored bodies of the bulls held up thick heads brandishing thick metal horns. Alana sketched them quickly.

The bulls did not emit steam or smoke. She had never seen such a device unless they were some sort of golems. "I don't see the means of locomotion," she whispered and wrote these thoughts beside her sketch.

"Nor I," Byronia said and handed her a quick sketch of the grounds. "The slave house is filled with humans. However, there's one Daosith adult, our two Fairsinge children, another Daosith child, plus an infant of undetermined race."

Alana clipped the drawing to her journal. The slave quarters, a rotting wood building with an open latrine on the east side of it and a shallow well to the west, stood behind a thick stone wall which separated it from the garden behind the family's stone house.

"Fight, steal or buy?" Alana asked.

"My uncle said to remain allies with the humans."

"Then we buy. How do I look?"

Alana wiped a bit of dirt off her tunic and checked her hair in her signaling mirror. The large twisted large bun was still intact. Alana covered her head with a translucent veil, the style of a married woman. As human maidens wore their hair in this Realm, Bryonia's two long plaits were intertwined with silk ribbons and tied to her scalp was a small woolen cap.

Byronia knocked on the intricately carved wooden door. The small peep window opened. "Yes?" The human male plastered a practiced smile on his powdered face which was surrounded by a powdered wig.

"Lady Alana of House Eyreid and Lady Byronia of House Silba seek Master and Mistress Kicuete for a business matter,: the young woman announced carefully enhancing her lyrical Fairsinge accent, in order to be treated by the rules of hospitality.

The human closed the window and unlatched the door. White dust fell upon the floor as he bowed. Was he too a slave or a paid servant? Would he fight for his master?

They were brought to a too-warm parlor where the butler directed the ladies to a padded divan. Once they were seated, he bowed his head. "The master and mistress will be with you shortly. May I offer you sherry?"

"Will you act as our taster, sir?" Byronia asked.

"While such things may be common in the Elf-lands, this is Dynion!"

"We beg pardon, good sir," Byronia said, her blue eyes looking wide and innocent.

The butler poured a cup of sherry and drew it to his lips. Then passed it to Alana who sipped it; he poured another and passed it to Byronia.

The master and mistress of the house appeared. He wore two or three layers of long silk robes which stretched over his belly while she wore a silk dress with a full skirt and headdress covering her long-twisted bun. They daintily placed themselves on the embroidered cushions of the divan across from where the ladies were seated.

"Thank you for seeing us," Alana said, keeping her voice soft. "I fear you interacted with our people in error and caused a divide amongst us."

"In error? We do not mean to offend the elfkin," the mistress said.

"Hence, we are here to make amends. You bought a twelve-year-old girl named Balrea and a ten-year-old boy Balhan a year ago at the slave auction. They are citizens of the Sildeir Province ruled by my Great and Wise Sister. We are here to collect them," Byronia said. "And there are two others who are the citizens of the Josael Province."

"I bought them fairly," the master said.

"We will pay fairly," Alana said.

The master waved his hand. The wigged butler came beside her divan. He bowed and gestured towards the door. "My lady, my ..."

Alana did not rise. He set his hand on her shoulder.

Byronia put a shivering hand on the saber on her belt.

"They were purchased fairly!" The woman's silk shoes squeaked on the wood floor as she stood.

"Yes, fairly," her husband repeated.

"At what price would you sell them?"

"Balrea has produced," the master said. "And the boy is a good worker."

Though Alana felt like screaming Balrea's a twelve-year-old girl, running her saber through the pair, and pissing upon their blood as it stained their fine carpets, she remained placid. "Ah. I see. Fear not, we will buy the produced child as well."

"They were purchased by the law! We need them." The woman of the house crossed the room, put her hand on Alana's arm and tugged upwards.

Alana remained seated.

"Yes, by the law," the master said, his face growing red.

The top of Byronia's silver blade sparkled in the low light of the parlor, and the wigged butler drew his blade. *Damn it!*

Alana rose and spun on her slippered foot. She knocked the mistress of the house to the floor and quickly disarmed the butler. She pressed her elbow against the artery in his neck. The butler fell forward, out cold. Byronia grasped him under the shoulders, carried him out the door and deposited him upon the hall floor. Alana looped the doorknob around a cabinet with a leather strap, so if the butler regained consciousness, he could not open the door.

Alana sat down again as placidly as before. "Forgive our outburst. My records say you paid thirty-two crowns for both Balrea and Balhan."

Byronia looked at her, opened her mouth and sat beside her. In her lyrical voice, she said, "I offer the bulk price of eight-seven Sovereigns of all four elfkin plus Balrea's offspring."

The husband and wife stammered, their soft, delicate hands pleaded. The man made out, "Eighty-seven, but..."

"Fine. An even hundred. Eighty-seven today and I'll have my Great and Wise Sister send another thirteen upon delivery. Though I'd like to watch you bleed for what you have done." Turning to Alana, Byronia said, still in the human tongue, "Our Empress would let them bleed for what they have done to our people." Using Empress instead of Doyenne. The girl was smart.

Since Byronia threatened them openly, Alana allowed the danger to linger in the air.

The humans leaned back on their embroidered divan cushions, not moving. Their eyes opened wide. Sweat drew trails in their powdered brows.

"My cousin is correct. We don't want to cheat you, nor did I come to open your flesh, though I have every right to do so," Alana said. "You may not buy or sell or keep any elfkin. Our people don't condone slavery," she lied. Plenty of the elfkin still condoned slavery.

The woman glanced at her husband and took his hand.

He opened his mouth, but only a panicked wheeze and spittle emerged.

"A hundred and forty is a fair price. It's a bulk purchase," the mistress of the house said quickly. "We will take the eighty-seven today, and I expect fifty-three in short order. And a ten percent late fee if I don't receive payment in, shall I say thirty days?"

"You will receive the second payment, once we land upon our shores. Thirty days should be sufficient," Alana said.

※

Elizabeth Guizzetti

Chapter 7
Daubmor Village in the Realm of Daouail

EOHAN SLAPPED A MOSQUITO WHICH BIT the bare flesh of his neck as he rode Cloudy up the rocky sun-dappled hillside. Cloudy swished her tail and neighed as Roark and Jaci got farther away. Though Cloudy was a large mare, she was carrying two riders and couldn't keep up with Jaci's pace.

Behind him, Kian clenched Eohan's waist a little tighter.

Eohan patted his brother's hand. "Remember what we taught you. Cloudy is a good horse."

"Yes, I remember," but Kian did not let go. Eohan pushed down his annoyance be remembering when he met Cloudy he was terrified of her too. And he had been a youth of eighteen, not a boy of eleven.

The wind carried the scent of smoke and elfkin over the rocks and into the valley. They had to pass through a village. An hour climb to the Guild, then they would be safe to rest before they would take a finely-kept Guild road to the Guild-controlled port on the other side of the mountain.

Roark pointed at the three and four-story stucco buildings perched upon the hillside. He gestured to Eohan. "There is no more cover -- we might as well ride in the open."

Roark led them around a large rock to ensure he was out of sight of the washer women standing upon the low red tile roof, lying laundry on iron railings enclosing a private courtyard.

On top of the hill, several white stucco buildings gleaming in the sun. Next, to the town gate, they passed a smaller building, smelling of feces and urine that people wearing ragged clothing entered and exited. The public latrine. The young men stopped to relieve themselves.

They moved to the nearby public fountain from which barefoot Daosith, Fairsinge and Fate women and children carried buckets of water into and up the stairs of the buildings. A drooling old Daosith man stared out into space, but his eyes followed the passers-by as they dropped coins into his cup.

The young men led the horses to the trough where the animals drank deeply. Roark and Eohan wiped down the mares as well as they could while still saddled. Kian hurried to the fountain again to refill the water sacks.

Four Daosiths -- a woman and three men -- stepped in front of Kian.

Eohan dropped the rag to the ground as the woman commanded in broken Fairsinger. "Name yourself, boy."

Kian cried out, "Han!"

Only seconds passed, but time slowed. The distance between Kian himself seemed insurmountable. Eohan knew he would never forget his little brother screaming his name.

Eohan said, "Roark!" as he dashed toward his brother.

"Looks like the little thief from the bounty to me," one of the men growled.

Eohan rushed towards the Daosith, drawing his claymore. Roark was behind him. Barefoot women and children raced away from the fountain carrying whatever water they had collected, blocking a clear path to Kian.

The first man lunged at Kian and caught hold of the loose tunic. The boy slipped to the ground and threw it off. The waterskins fell to the ground. The man reached for Kian again but never reached him as Eohan barreled into him. They tumbled onto the dirt road.

"Only injure!" Roark shouted. It didn't matter what Roark said, Eohan ensured the man who touched his brother never took another breath as his heavy blade entered his chest, crashing against his ribs and hitting his lungs.

"For the love of the Goddess!" Roark cried. His companion might be annoyed Eohan killed someone, but there was no time to think that now. He sized up the next three opponents. They didn't seem experienced enough to be from Guild though they were probably hired as muscle from time to time.

The woman grabbed hold of Kian and pulled him off his feet. Careful not to hit Kian, Roark slashed his sword down in front of her, forcing her to stop short. With the knowledge Roark would protect Kian, Eohan took on the other two.

Eohan punched his next opponent to the dirt. The man staggered back from the blow.

His fist slammed into his opponent's face again. His knuckles felt the bones underneath flesh give.

❋

WITH ONE HAND ON THE SCRUFF OF KIAN'S tunic, the woman and pulled an iron cudgel from her belt. Kian tried to swing a fist at her, but, dancing on his tiptoes, he couldn't get power. He tried to kick. "Thieves! Murderer!" she screamed.

Roark never looked towards Kian; his eyes were focused only on his opponents, yet the look of determination as he advanced washed the terror from Kian's heart.

The woman swung her cudgel through the air forcing Roark to retreat two steps.

Another man flanked Roark, but faster than Kian could see, the older apprentice spun, sliced an arch through the air and cut low towards the man's thigh who fell to the ground screaming.

Roark's back was to her; the woman swung again.

Kian realized each attack towards Roark pushed his captor off-balance. He waited until the correct moment. He kicked her in the knee. She crumpled onto the dirt, losing her weapon and her hold on him. He was free!

With his unburdened hand, Roark shoved Kian towards Cloudy. "Run!"

Quicker than expected, the woman clambered to her feet and pushed Roark onto the ground. Dust rose as he hit the road. She buried his head in the dirt with her knee in his back. He spat out muddy spit. Roark yanked his elbow back, rolled until her weight lifted off of him.

Kian was supposed to run but saw an abandoned ceramic pot. He hauled it up in the air.

Kian dashed the pot to the woman's head. With a loud crash, ceramic shattered. The woman fell to the ground.

Stunned, Kian didn't move.

"Go," Roark shouted.

"Did you see what I did!"

"Yes! Go."

The boy grabbed the dropped water skins and raced to Cloudy. Roark hurried to aid Eohan who was still fighting the last man. He didn't make it there when Eohan's huge fist hit the temple of his opponent, and the man fell into the dirt.

"Go, go."

Roark turned toward Kian and lifted him onto Jaci's back. He leapt up behind him.

Jaci reared. Kian feared falling but tried to hold tight. One of the men, now recovering, threw a stone towards them. Before it hit Kian, Roark blocked it with his arm.

Eohan was on Cloudy. She scurried down the road.

Like the noble Martlets in one of Pa's old stories, Roark tossed three coppers in the air, they landed with a plink, plink, plink in the old man's cup.

Ahead of him, Cloudy cantered down the dirt road, and Eohan was forced to make a wide turn to miss a woman scolding her child.

"Lowest Realm!" Roark's turn was not as clean, but the child's scream and the mother's swear let him know that they were unhurt by his closeness.

Kian glanced back to be sure. He wasn't sure he'd ever forget the horrible open-jawed look of absolute terror on the woman's face though she screamed obscenities after them. It reminded him too much of the look on his mother's face when she tried to hold him tight, while the slavers ripped them apart.

"Don't worry, they were scared, but not hurt."

Behind them, three out of the four were getting to their feet.

He didn't know if they had horses. And Jaci carried two.

Roark centered their balance by moving his feet directly below his hips and pulled Kian closer to his chest. Kian glanced up, but Roark's eyes focused on the open road. He squeezed Jaci. She raced towards Cloudy and easily overtook the other horse.

The road became a blur beneath their feet.

As Jaci jumped over a log, a small whimper escaped his lips, but he refused to complain. He squeezed his eyes shut. *Roark, please don't let me fall.*

✳

The Guild House of Laithmor in the Realm of Daouail

HORSES HOOVES POUNDED THE DIRT ROAD —only wide enough for a single cart. At times, Roark felt Jaci slipping in the loose soil, but his mare pushed on without his prodding. It was only another twenty miles or so, and they would be at the Guild House of Laithmor. Behind him, Cloudy, unburdened, kept pace.

They crested a small plateau. Looking at the sweat on Jaci's neck, he worried about Daouails' two suns beating down upon them. After this temporary leveling, the road would still climb. "Ho there, girl."

In response, Eohan stopped Cloudy.

"We ought to slow the pace," Roark dismounted and helped Kian to the ground. "We're safe enough. I'm worried for the mares."

"Agreed," Eohan said.

"Agreed," Kian repeated.

Roark scanned the hillside with his eyeglass. Below there was still no one following. The villagers who attacked them must not have the means to care for horses. That meant they were not members of the Guild. Thank the Goddess for that. Eohan would never forgive Roark if his little brother were killed.

Above, Guild harvesters were collecting the dubfeid's shedding on the open hillside as the herd of long-haired black deer with golden antlers grazed.

The three picked their way up the hillside to the valley. Used to the Guild presence, the dubfeid ignored the young men and their horses as they ignored the harvesters. After a few hundred feet, Kian gasped with every step and fell slightly behind, but he did not complain even as damp sweat coated his tunic and his head drooped. The youngest apprentice kept shuffling forward until the ground leveled again.

Roark led the way to the keep built into a rocky hillside of black and white speckled granite. Larger than the Guild House at Olentir, unbroken spires of the keep reached towards the heavens slicing the larger of the two suns in half. It seemed peaceful, but Roark knew within tiny unseen holes, guards watched for approaching violence. They crossed under the first gate where the party was welcomed by the hooded sentries.

Cupping his hand, Roark touched his thumb to his forefinger and gestured across his chest. "We're the apprentices of War Ender Alana, seeking shelter and audience with Guild Surgeon Seweryn if he's here. Or another surgeon if he's not."

The guard gestured in kind and opened the door. Another saluted and asked if he could care for the horses.

"Indeed."

He wrote out numbers on a slip of paper and said, "Stables fifteen and sixteen."

"Thank you."

Jaci neighed until Roark patted her nose. Cloudy nuzzled her way in too. Then followed the Guild Stablehand towards the stables. They knew the routine.

Once inside, Roark winced at the sound of Kian's footsteps on the stone floor. He didn't want to embarrass the boy, so he said nothing, though he imagined Eohan carrying him on his back. He led them first into the refectory where chefs moved between the long heavy wooden tables with platters of food. However, he didn't want to draw more attention to himself, he nodded his head to the music. Candles flickered in overhead lanterns casting moving shadows on the bright-limed plaster which covered most of the walls.

They slipped onto wooden stools before an empty table. A group of Daosith men sang a traditional song in the corner. He listened to the story and wondered if he should translate it for Eohan's whose Daosithian was still shoddy -- except the few words of love he had picked up from Nalla. From the little he had heard, Kian knew some Daosithian as was necessary for his former situation.

Roark gestured at a server and in Daosithian, said, "Food, water only please."

Quickly, a server dropped off cups of crystal clear water. Another dropped off bread and ceramic bowls each with a young hen stewed with sour fruit.

Roark couldn't relax. A guild member was supposed to be above nationality, Great House, or species, but rules don't follow an intelligent species heart. He didn't even know if he could trust Lord Seweryn if he learned Roark committed a regicide amongst the Daosithians. As with the Fairsinge Guild Members, most Guild members in Daouail were nobleborn. Eohan blended in somewhat, but it was obvious. Kian ate too quickly. His fingers kept fidgeting over the cutlery as if it burned him.

Across the table, a Daosithian woman whispered to a man. Her tawny eyes did not move from Roark's face. He didn't think he knew her.

"Let's find a free cabinet. They're this way."

They crossed stone pavers in the open yard to the barracks. Roark still felt as if everyone was looking at them.

They entered the long hallway. Most of the doors were marked with a symbol. Roark led them to a blank door, knocked just in case, then opened the door. It whined on its hinges. He peeked inside. The room was empty except the large bed and trunk. The stone floor is covered by a jute carpet which thankfully would muffle any sound Kian made. He took the chalk and drew the eagle in a diamond for House Eyreid. He mimicked Alana's hand, hoping everyone would assume the War Ender was with them.

"Let's get a few hours sleep and get out of here," Eohan said softly.

"You notice the couple?"

"Yes."

Roark pressed his ear to the wooden door and listened for footsteps in the hallway. There were none to be heard -- not that meant anything -- nearly all Guild members walked in silence after their first month of training -- even the stewards. He slipped a mirror under the door, the hallways were crowded, but silent. He was in a Guild House, surrounded by assassins, intelligent surveyors, surgeons, guards, War Enders -- all walking without sound. *Alana trusted me, and I failed her, it was a mistake to come here with Kian. I took the wrong path.*

"But we're here," Eohan said from the bed behind him. "We all need sleep, and the horses need to be rested."

As he turned around, Roark realized Eohan had read his mind.

"I don't need to read your mind to see what you are thinking," the older apprentice said.

Roark smiled wanly. "And if they come for us?"

"Being unrested won't help."

Roark lay on the other side of Kian who had already fallen asleep. He whispered, "I thought taking a Guild ship was best, but now ..." He looked up towards the bare ceiling and tried to come up with something. "Since they are looking for an arena prizefighter, maybe your body is giving us away."

"I can slouch more."

"Yes! And what if we padded your stomach? Give you a paunch? With cosmetics, I can make you look older. You can pretend to be the master." Roark's thought was interrupted by a letter slipped under the door. Roark went to retrieve it.

You want to see me? Kajsa holds Chamber 17. It was reported the person who killed the Empress also stole the ruby around her throat -- or if they didn't, they are fools.

S

"We're saved or sarded. Unsure which," Roark said. "Seweryn and Kajsa are here."

"Doriel, too?" Eohan shook his brother's shoulder.

"I'd assume so."

"But I just fell asleep," Kian muttered, then sat up straight and jumped off the bed, close to his brother.

"We're still safe, I think," Roark said. "But we need to see some people."

The three apprentices emptied the trunk of extra bedding and stuffed it under the blankets, so it looked as if they were still under the covers, carefully gathered their gear and crept down the long hallway to one of the larger chambers. They passed an old woman sweeping the floor. They could not see her dark skin under her hood, but her silver eyes watched them.

Roark knocked on the door of Chamber 17.

"Roark, Eohan, it's good to see you, and you must be Kian. Your brother spoke of you often." Lord Seweryn, said, standing and opening his arms wide. His silver hair was freshly washed, and laundry hung on the line. His obsidian skin caught the light and Roark was surprised Seweryn was sort of handsome when he wasn't struggling with the Soldier's Melancholy. Though she was nearly twenty years his senior, Seweryn, and Alana even had a short love affair, he could almost see what his aunt had seen in him.

Behind him at the table sat Lady Kajsa, a dwarf swordswoman and by her side as always was Doriel

Angrock: her brother-in-law and brother-in-arms. Their golden hair and full beards were neatly plaited. Doriel was shining armor, and Kajsa was sharpening her claymore. Though unsure of their intentions, Roark was glad to see them. Kajsa was once Alana's apprentice.

"Don't haunt a doorway, come inside," Kajsa said. Her rich blue eyes glimmered in the candlelight, and her cheeks looked rosy, but the shriek of the whetstone against the long blade unnerved him.

Roark gestured to the other two. They entered behind him.

"Sit and eat -- there is nothing in your cups but spring water, though my brother and I'll still be partaking of mead."

"Thank you, my lady," Roark inclined his head. "How did you know?"

"I overheard you in the rectory," Kajsa said. "So is it true? The game had Alana's mark on it -- except for the stolen ruby."

"I didn't steal a ruby," Roark snapped. "Nothing of value!"

Doriel flicked his ear. "Shhh. Do you want to be heard?"

"Yes, we did the regicide with Guild approval -- and I didn't steal anything except some trifles off a dressing table to make it look like a robbery."

"What type of trifles?"

Roark opened his bag and pulled out an enameled face powder box, an ivory-handled brush, and other items off the dressing table. "The only thing Eohan stole was his brother."

"And I also stole a kitchen knife. To get him out of the chains," Kian whispered.

"Thank you for a full accounting, dear." Kajsa set aside the sword and whetstone and reached towards him. "Elfkin youth seem so fragile. You are but eleven summers?"

"Yes, milady."

For her outward loving demeanor, Roark already guessed she wanted to study him. "We heard the arena brute was chained, real lock?"

"Yes," Eohan said.

"And Kian picked it? Without any training at all?"

"Only kitchen work, my lady. I was lucky to be skilled in my parents' trades when I was sold."

"No doubt. Injuries?"

Kian shook his head.

Roark hoped the others would not consider that a lie. "Nothing of note," he answered. "He'll live by a life of his choosing."

"What a gift you were given, Kian." Something shifted behind Seweryn's eyes.

Kian sits between two people who can kill in an instant. Maybe, it's wrong to trust them. "Don't hurt him!" Roark cried.

Kian started to rise, but Lady Kajsa held his arm. "Sit."

He sat back down, frozen in place.

Doriel clamped his hand upon Eohan. "Trust us. Don't do something stupid."

"I killed the Empress alone. I poisoned her quickly and strangled her dead body to hide how, but I didn't steal anything of real value –some shiny trinkets from the dressing table, I swear on my rights of a Martlet. Eohan only rescued his brother. Don't hurt them! Even Alana is innocent."

Laughter burst out of the dwarfs' lips at his last statement.

Seweryn smiled. "A jester's talent. We had no idea, I'll make a note of it."

Eohan and Roark met eyes and chuckled uncomfortably. Kian was still frozen.

"Your loyalty is admirable, but you really ought to work on not showing it for their sakes," Doriel said. "As long as it doesn't affect our pay, we aren't interested in your jobs when we are not around."

"However, Lord Corwin is interested speaking to you about the job and seeing the boy," Kajsa said.

"Why'd he send Alana away?"

"Ask him yourself." Seweryn set up a silver sounding bowl with cool, clear water.

Kajsa sprinkled an iron-red powder into the water and slipped her hand into it. "House Master Corwin, we found them. Or more accurately they found us."

A thin, wrinkled, sneering face appeared in the water. "So, nearly-a-lord Roark, how do you feel about your first regicide?"

"I was honored for the opportunity." A safe answer when talking to the House Master.

"You'll be honored for another, I suppose."

Roark's mouth went dry, but he nodded.

"Legend says the stolen ruby..."

"But I didn't..."

Corwin gestured, and Kajsa slapped the side of Roark's head. She hadn't hit him hard, but he shut his mouth.

"As I was saying, this stolen ruby of legend gave the Empress a long life and the wisdom to rule. If the jewel works, we need to study the technology. I've seen your curiosity in such things."

Roark chewed his bottom lip and decided to name it. "Was the Empress a necromancer?"

"No. She kept one on retainer. We know little about the necromancer other than she was a Daosith woman named Daena. Age eighty-seven. A third cousin or some other minor relations to House Josael."

"If you wanted us to get this jewel, why did you send Lady Alana away?"

"Because Alana claims you're worthy to start your Journey. If you are able to find this illegal technology with Guild resources, I will not stand in the way of your advancement."

Roark felt twisted by madness: he needed to get Eohan and Kian to Fairdhel, but if he started his Journey... "Would the bounty go away if we find this jewel?"

"One of you slap some sense into that boy!"

Kajsa did as Corwin commanded, but like before she put no power into her blow.

Corwin went on: "You committed regicide, boy! The bounty will live on forever. However, from all reports, the new Empress is well loved by her people. Most importantly, no one except Alana and the people in this room know you did the deed.

"If this opportunity frightens you: sell the other two boys to the younger Empress and save yourself the trouble."

Corwin's words ripped into Roark's heart and beside him, Eohan's hand formed a fist. *It's a trick. How would Alana handle this?* As soon as he thought of his aunt, a plan started to form. "House Master Corwin, what are the consequences if we find the Empress's ruby and bring it to you. If we found another a ruby of the same make and quality and replaced it. If this second ruby was returned to the Empress by a noble dwarf lady and her support staff along with the bodies of two slaves..."

Beside him, Kian squeaked.

"Don't be stupid and don't interrupt," Roark growled though unlike Corwin, he wouldn't slap Kian or order Kajsa to. That would be no better than bullying. "Well, would the young Empress know the difference?"

Corwin sneer almost became a smile. "Probably not."

"What resources do I have at my disposal? Is Lady

Kajsa unemployed?"

"I suppose, but what can an apprentice pay a journeywoman at the end of her decade -- only seventy-three days before she becomes a practicing War Ender. Her fees are quite expensive for a boy such as yourself."

Roark was tired of being referred to as a boy. (Well, from everyone but Alana who said boys when she grouped her apprentices together with affection.) "That'll be my problem."

"Indeed."

"House Master Corwin, I accept this opportunity, but I require one more thing in payment."

"Which is?"

"This is a test for Eohan, Kian, and I. You won't stand in the way of my advancement nor my friends' advancement within the Guild."

"You've traveled with Alana for too long. She softened your brutality."

"Perhaps, but it's my price. I don't come cheap either."

"Very well," Corwin said, "You will start your Decade if you procure this technology for me and survive, and I will not stand in the way of these two commoners when they are ready if they survive."

The image of Corwin disappeared from the water.

Knees trembling, Roark sank in a nearby chair. He hated showing such weakness, but he did not have control of his body.

"So, we've never worked for an apprentice," Kajsa said, stroking her beard. "Out of curiosity, how will you pay my fee?"

Roark whispered, "You, three journeypersons, get the whole bounty if you help us. I leave it to you to divide it in whatever way seems fair to you."

"Solid price there, but how will you live?" Kajsa asked.

"Alana gave me a little money, and I still have my House allowance if need be. It has been enough so far for the three of us. We've been keeping to the woods."

Kajsa tapped her knee with her fingers. "Yet, you were seen and killed a man in Daubmor."

"Yes, my lady, I killed him," Eohan said. "I lost my temper after he grabbed Kian."

"It wouldn't be uncommon for two men to dump a boy slowing them down," Kajsa said. "We could procure a boy's body, bring it to House Josael, get more information about the jewel and perhaps even get partial bounty. Once it's known I'm after the bounty, it should take some heat off you."

Roark glanced at Eohan. "That's a good idea. Let's do that."

"How did you plan to procure a youth's body, and later a man's body for Eohan?" Seweryn said.

Roark opened his mouth, but no sound came out. He had no idea. *Think like Alana...*

Eohan jumped in. "We think, my lord when it is time we could procure bodies from an arena graveyard for me. But for a corpse my brother's size, I'm not sure."

"Sadly, children also die in the arena every day." Seweryn pulled out a measuring ribbon and his journal. His voice was soft, sad and distant. Roark hoped he would keep bathing for a while.

※

Chapter 8
Port Dentwort in the Realm of Dynion

"**A** MESSAGE FOR YOU, LADY ALANA." LILLIA carried a seagull into the Guild cabin and set the bird on the table.

Alana unwrapped the scroll. Inside was a brief message from Roark about the job Corwin had set them on. She bit the inside of her cheek, refusing to show emotion in front of Byronia -- or swear about her beloved uncle's conduct. *It is his duty as House Master to see when promotions are due.* She reminded herself, but since Corwin was against any commoner in the high ranks, she did not believe he was doing this to help her nephew and his friends.

Of course, as she was in Dentwort, she might call on Edar and get more information. She fed the gull a few grapes from the table. "Might you stay until I finish the night's work, my friend? I might have something for you to send back."

The gull bobbed its head and side-eyed the grapes. Balhan wandered over and put his hand out. The gull sidestepped to him and peeked over his hand.

"Apparently he likes grapes," Alana said. "I'll be back in a few hours; mind the gull for me."

"Yes, milady," Balhan took one from the bunch

and gave it a grape.

Looking back down at her list, she spoke in the pre-schism language of the elfkin nobility so the rescued slaves wouldn't understand. "Now, where were we? Edar said this name is a pimp. I shall kill him I think."

"Someday the Guild will crucify you for killing the wrong person," Byronia said in the same tongue. "We might try buying the girl from her pimp."

Alana slowly dressed in the weave then wrapped a cloak round her body. "In this case, killing is better. This girl disappears with us tonight, and we sail back to Olentir. I must get back to the boys."

Alana saw the children watching her as she took a soot pencil and covered the flesh around her eyes. Her hands were practiced, but she still checked the mirror. Alana carefully adjusted her scabbards. Her saber on her right hip, two daggers on the left. Two throwing knives were knotted to her left thigh, and on her right, was a small ration of hardtack, and a needle and thread, and coin.

"Good journey," Byronia said, before turning to the group of rescued slaves playing a game of hafal in the corner.

Alana followed the beach to a cobbled boat ramp which led to grime and urine-infused clay buildings set with heavy timbers where Edar never ventured but knew by reputation. Alana crept towards the center of the buildings where wooden racks covered in salted fish lay smoking, and down a darkened alleyway to an inn and brothel.

Alana perched in the dim shadows. A few drunks walked by singing arm in arm.

Her muscles twitched from excitement. Her mind felt a tingling heat as she waited for the child to appear. She loved this type of work. It was much better than war ending where even innocent blood flowed at times. Only the guilty were bled on rescue missions.

Alana watched Caraine, daughter of Ylsabet, and the pimp leave the brothel and cross the alley towards a filth-encrusted inn.

Caraine's—whose record put her at thirteen—tri-pointed ears pierced with golden chains which wrapped behind her head, but the jewelry was the only thing colorful about her attire. On her body, she wore a stained slip. The man holding the chains dressed in gaudy striped linens that smelled like fish. Her eyes were orbs of expressionless gravity, though her mouth pretended to smile. Rage boiled up in Alana.

Careful not to step in the light from the windows, she followed before they went into the inn for the night's business. Alana leaped from the shadows with a knife in each hand. Her right blade entered the man's neck smoothly, as did her left.

Clutching on the spurting wound, the man fell forward in pain and dropped the girl's chain. Caraine spun around, yelling in confusion.

Alana slapped a hand over the girl's mouth and pulled her into the shadows before the man dropped on her. Blood spurted from the wounds. Within seconds, the man stopped moving.

Holding the girl. Alana whispered, "Should we finish it?"

"Finish?" the girl whimpered.

"Ensure he cannot be recognized and look for valuables," Alana instructed. Holding the girl by the scruff of her dress, Alana spun her around and removed her hand. "Child, we need to get you away from here less they think you did this. Do as I bade you," Alana asked.

"I don't have to go back to the brothel?" The girl hugged herself.

"Surely you've heard of the Martlets?

"The Martlets?"

"The elf nobility who travel the Realms and help the broken. Would you enjoy stabbing him? I could loan you a knife, dearling."

With tears in her eyes, Caraine took the knife, spit on the man's corpse and made one glancing blow to his chest with a quiet scream. Her second blow punctured the flesh of his stomach. Trembling, Caraine handed the knife back to Alana.

"Now, I must ask you an important question, and you must answer truthfully,"

"Yes, milady?"

"Is there any other elfkin, whether they be Fairsinge, Daosith or Fate, who dwell in the brothel? I'll rescue them too."

Caraine shook her head. "I never saw any of our people. Only humans and the occasional dwarf who visited the inn."

"And the other prostitutes?"

"There were three, all human girls."

"Stay here."

Alana crept back to the brothel. Inside, two girls cried while the eldest girl paced. She knocked on the door.

The eldest girl shooed the other girls behind a curtain before she peered out the window.

Lowering her voice to what she hoped was deep as a man's, she grumbled, "Caraine and your pimp are dead. I bring you this to buy your freedom." Alana dropped a bag of coin through the window and walked away. Behind her, she heard joyous laughter.

Caraine rocked back and forth holding her arms tight.

"Let's get you back to Macotir."

Alana rested her arm over the girl's shoulders. She stayed under Alana's arm as they walked to the shore and headed north.

After a time, they came to a freshwater stream leading up a ravine, slicing the beach in two. "Best to not enter the ship in the weave or blood on your hands, child," Alana said softly. "The other children might be frightened."

Cara washed her hands. "Other children?"

"House Silba's Martlet and I are trying to find all who were stolen from Sildeir Province."

"You are not of Sildeir?"

"No, I'm Lady Alana of House Eyreid."

"Then why help me?"

"The Martlets ride for all our people; it is our sorrow we did not find you sooner."

Caraine looked at her feet. "Do you know what happened to my mother and sisters?"

"Many died on the ship, but some have been rescued. If they lived, they're in Sildeir or Eyredeir. We'll find out what happened to her at least. What's her name?

"Wisewoman Ylsabet."

"There is a wisewoman in Eyredeir; she buried a babe after I rescued her."

Caraine's eyes filled with tears.

"Once we're aboard the ship, you are going to get a nice warm bath. I'm going to show you a mark, and you can tell me if it is your mother's."

✳

"I NEED A REMEDY AND INFORMATION," Alana said to Edar.

"For yourself?" He ushered her into his cozy cottage. She could smell the sharp scent of vinegar upon his silks. He gestured at the gull. "Or your bird?"

"No, a young girl from the brothel district. Elfkin."

"I've a less effective remedy suitable for a pregnant girl that won't harm the babe if she wants it," Edar said softly. "Or something stronger, but she will lose the child."

"We don't know she's pregnant, only malnourished, misused and itches. Our steward bathed her in oil, but she still itches. She's only been with humans and dwarves since she arrived on these shores. Guild doctors treat wounds well enough, but know nothing about diseases."

"And the Guild has always been a self-righteous about medical technologies," Edar said not hiding his disdain.

"Our inequities are my shame."

"Your shame doesn't save lives," Edar said.

"You believe you understand morality?" Alana asked.

"Better than you. There is a new disease going around the brothels and slave ships, but the apothecaries haven't defined how its spread yet. An internal round of quicksilver and holy wood has proven effective. She must take the first dose in the morning light of tomorrow and again at night. Finish in twenty-eight days. Is she well enough to spread a tonic on infected skin?"

"Yes, and I've a steward caring for the children until we arrive back in Olentir."

"Good. I'll make enough for all the children to bath in twice. I suggest you, the steward, and Lady Byronia, and anyone else who's been around the child, to also wash in case its spread by bad air or parasite."

He picked some chamomile from his window box then pulled out a pot of a sharp smelling resin. He boiled water and dropped it in the pot. "Give each child a slice of this cheese. It's made with an old pre-schism remedy called Penicillin."

Alana brightened. "I've heard of that. How much?"

He counted out the slices and weighed out each ingredient. "Fifty-eight Sovereigns and three chips."

Alana gave him the amount requested. "I also

need some information about a ruby."

"Don't know much about jewels."

"You might know something about this one. It was created for the Empress of Daouail by a necromancer."

Edar glanced away. He obviously knew something. She kept going: "The Empress is dead, and it has been stolen. Her granddaughter who succeeded her wants it returned."

"Why would you think I know anything about it?"

"It's quite strange, but in my travels, I learned though the seven realms are vast, small connections often intertwine over and over again. You and the creator of the gem are both necromancers."

Edar nodded, still not meeting her eye, and wandered towards the stove.

"When you bought a slave, you bought an elfkin for his blood. What would you like for information?"

"I'll give that freely for your continued presence," Edar said.

"What?"

"Stay 'til morning."

She took a step back, surprised by the request.

"Don't be afraid. I don't want anything unseemly or base. When I'm flush with blood, I miss companionship. Hold my hand if you can bear the cold, but I won't even touch you if you don't permit it."

"Aren't you afraid I have a parasite?"

"Lady, one benefit of being undead is parasites which desire your warm blood do not like the taste of mine."

Alana touched the cold hand of the undead. Other than a longing for blood due to the constant fear of death, Edar wasn't a bad man compared to others she had known.

"Should I put on the kettle?" he asked.

"Please."

"And can I get anything for your bird?"

"Just information so I might send her to Roark, who waits for my word."

Waiting for the kettle to whistle, Edar opened his window and picked a bunch of chamomile from the sill. "The ruby is not a ruby. It's deep red like a ruby, but it's a piece of quartz, cut and polished to look like a fine gem and filled with blood."

"A remedy?"

"No, just the bearer's blood. The Empress sacrifices a few drops of blood to the jewel each night, and the jewel kept her alive and gave her the wisdom to think through any problem for her people. Oddly, it might have even kept that rake of a consort alive since she was too wise to be perturbed by his actions."

"You know of him?"

"Only through Madam Grunkit's words. She said, though your boys looked as if they had murder in their eyes, you were fair-minded and understanding to their plight."

"If I have to rescue another slave boy from them, I might not be."

"They seemed aware of that as am I." The kettle whistled, and Edar poured boiling water over the chamomile. After holding the cold dead hand, the warmth of the tea was welcome.

Alana didn't reply until Edar filled the silence. "I miss my mother. Thysta was a great remedy woman, so wise in our ways, but she refused to walk as a lich. Like you, dear lady, she has had many apprentices, but they all eventually scatter and follow the winds."

"Did she carve the stone or did Daena?"

"Together. My mother cast the spell for wisdom. Daena came to us as a lovestruck page assigned to the Mayor's House. She needed wisdom in the worse way."

"Daena was a page?"

"If the elfkin trusted you enough with one of their young, you were trustworthy. And for a silk merchant, trust is invaluable. It is said that the trust of the elfkin built Port Dentwort. Did you ever live with a human family?"

Now she had some idea that Edar walked this Realm for at least eighty years, perhaps even longer. Sending the younger siblings to Human lands fell out of fashion before her generation. She said, "My House is too far north to participate in such honors. I was taught by my beloved Uncle Caden. He bade me join the Guild and hoped we'd work together for many years in Intelligence. However, I wished to wander like the Martlet's of olde and became a War Ender. Also, I was in love with a young man who also ended wars."

"Did it last?"

Alana knew by giving of herself, Edar would open up, but she also knew he would not judge her. She was a War Ender; he was a Necromancer. They both dealt in death. "Our love lasted less than a year into my journey, but he is so dashing, handsome and intelligent, we met often, and he sired my daughter."

"You still find him dashing?"

She laughed. "Well, I suppose, we're both a bit long in the tooth to be considered dashing, but he's brilliant. At times, infuriatingly so."

"Grandchildren?"

"No, my daughter fell in battle."

"I'm sorry to hear that. Do you believe she has been resurrected back to the nobility as the priests tell us?"

Alana shook her head. She believed in nothing, but her foresight. And foresight had failed her in regard to Saray. Witnessing the priest lay oils upon her daughter's corpse had crushed her in ways she hadn't imagined was possible. "Saray was a great protector of children,

75

so I'd like to think so. However, during my mourning, I wandered into the family crypt many nights, opened her coffin and watched as her corpse bloat and fall into putrescence as with every other iron-blooded creature in the Realms."

"Why?"

"I wanted to be with her in death since I failed her in life. If I had only gone back to Eyredeir instead of remaining on the job, Saray might have lived. The Guild would have charged me with negligence for leaving in the middle of the war, but the worst they could have ever done is crucify me. I'd have accepted that fate gladly if she had lived -- and I believe her father feels the same."

"Most parents would. I'm sorry I upset you." Edar hurried to his cupboard. He found a handkerchief and refilled their cups.

"You did not. Teaching helps fill the hole in my heart, but I still dream of her at times. Do you have children?"

Edar shook his head. "My wife died in childbirth: twins. My son died with her. My daughter lived only for nine days. The marriage was arranged, but I enjoyed my wife's company and mourned her. Daena was before my wife, but we were friends."

"I suppose, Mayor Kleidmacher — who wouldn't have been the mayor yet — was dashing."

"Hence his father, the former Mayor Kleidmacher, sent her to live with us. If there was a dignitary in town, she went back to the Mayor's house, then sent back here.

"When young, I believe their love was true.

"At first, David visited often. As mayor's sons often do, David had responsibilities to his family to marry well, to produce a human son, to continue his family's legacy. He visited less and less until his engagement was announced. I tried to be a friend, even a lover when she ached for that, but her heart grew cold in her sorrow.

Eventually, she traveled back to live as a companion to her cousin." Edar blinked the tears from his eyes and Alana squeezed his cold hand.

Alana knew he'd tell her more, but he'd hate himself if he felt he betrayed Daena. Better for Alana to keep the ally -- and better for Edar to not face eternity with regret. She spared him.

"When did you decide to live forever?"

His eyes lifted again. "As my mother grew old, I grew more interested. I heard of the Lich 'spell' and decided to see if it worked. It did. Why do you ask; want to live forever?"

"Death shall find me. However, I've apprentices to train and slaves to rescue. Too much to do."

She scrawled all of her notes on the back of the parchment Roark sent, then stuffed it into the Gull's scroll carrier.

"Be well, my friend," she said to the gull and carried it to the window. Its long white wings flapped as it took flight and flew off into the night.

"I never understood your people."

"Do you know the story of how the Martlets came to be?"

"Only after the Schism, the elfkin nobility followed a strict line of succession based on birth order. To keep the younger siblings out of the way, your people send them on quests or to the Guild."

"That's true. There's a story if you'd like to hear it."

"How much is true?"

Probably none of it...." She recited, "Our people's history is measured in multiple epochs, and we know there have been more than one Schism. Before the first, it is said, time moved slower in the Realm of the Fair.

"The Sun wanted children. She walked our land and took elfin men. The land became scorched, and these men died of course, because what man could bear the heat of the sun? Hearing our people cry, Lancia, the wisest of the thirteen Goddesses, formed a scythe from the strongest metal and stone. She cut the Sun, carving out the little suns which orbit her.

"Though the sun had lost part of herself, she had gained something too. She went back to the heavens, and our Realm grew green and prosperous.

"In this first epoch, thirteen Great Houses were created for the thirteen Goddesses along with a high house built upon our tallest mountain which was the home of the Sun and her children.

"In the second epoch, the Goddesses and the Sun lived in their great Houses which my people built, but the people grew weary. Siblings created war upon one another for thrones throwing our Realm into chaos. One by one, the thirteen houses fell until there was only one left. Yet even that wasn't enough. In the last generation before the first Schism, five siblings each vyed for the throne. Their people suffered.

Two died in battle, and their last monarch of the Fair cursed the three remaining. But war is always shifting and either the last monarch, or one of these three burned the land until our Realm shattered into three: Fairdhel, Fatedhel, and Daouail.

"The other three could see each other and their armies, but we could no longer touch. No longer fight.

"Worse, the last monarch of the Fair and realized they tore open the veil to Dynion and Larcia. She did not know when your people would come, only you would be coming. As she was in Daouail, she found her last surviving child and began the change there.

"Unfortunately, the child tried to rebel, he or she was struck from history, and the monarch searched for a gentle soul to rule. But that is another story n...

"After finding this gentle soul, she redistributed

wealth throughout Daouail's original thirteen provinces and told her thirteen wisest advisers to rebuild.

"Her own house was built on the tallest mountain. She and the girl who would become the first Empress created a line of succession: The first rules the great house, the second rules the priesthood, the third wanders for the good of our people, the fourth strengthens the house through marriage or alliance. Any child after the fourth go to our allies' homes and study their ways so we may strengthen our culture."

"Like Daena," Edar said.

"Yes. Though those first generations were just in Daouail. Until the Larcian Dwarves and Gnomes developed InterRealm Ships, the walls between our people were insurmountable."

"Obviously."

"When the Daouail found the Fairsingers on scorched and broken land, intermarriage was crucial.

"The Larcian's were explorers, looking for adventure and gold, but they are also an ancient species as old as stone and have the wisdom of the mountains. More wisdom than we did anyway. They spoke of the need for peace which brings pleasure and wealth. They sought our riches, including the elfkin, who were gifted with foresight amongst the nobility. Daouail feared we too would become a commodity in a generation; the line of succession came to our shores."

Edar nodded. "In our version of the tale, our people caused the holes in the veil. We could see the Larcians but couldn't touch them most of the time. They and we created the Guild, and when the elfkin came, they were assimilated into our ways."

Alana laughed. "And in our stories, we assimilated you and the Guild to our ways."

Edar sighed. "All the old traditions are falling out of favor. Peaceful trade, my arse. Famine moved across

Dynion and slavery followed. Our laws once only allowed for criminals to be enslaved, but within a generation, slavery became an industry here. And no elfkin pages in the mayor's house or any of our people's houses."

Alana nodded. "In the elfkin Realms, many thirdborns claim Martlet and vow service but don't serve anyone. There is no real requirement anymore. They stay home -- fearful they might be attacked at any moment."

"By who?"

"I don't know. Last year I stopped a war between the Telchine and Dwarves. I feel something's changing, but that may be the ramblings of a frightened old woman."

"Do you believe this change is because the traditions are dying or because the Guild has tightened its grip on technology, slowing us further?"

"I don't know, but I must fight the symptoms until I find the answer and destroy the cause with my dying breath if I can."

"You speak as if you are doomed."

"I don't know how I'll die or when, but I've seen the future beyond my death. If my last service can be to the good of my House or the betterment of the Realms, I'd die happy."

Edar raised his cup. "I was glad to know you and taste your blood while you walked in this form. As I plan to walk for centuries and see the fate of my people and yours, may I recognize your valiant spirit in your next life, Alana of House Eyreid. And may your idiotic glorious noble death be quick, since it is unlikely to be painless."

They gently clinked their teacups together. "I'm glad I know you, Edar Candlewick." She leaned towards him and took his hand again. The teacup had warmed his hand enough that it was not deathly cold, just cooler than she.

※

Chapter 9
Morcon Arena in the Realm of Daouail

EOHAN FOLLOWED THE OTHERS INTO THE village of make-shift daub and stick buildings which surrounded the large stone arena. The beating of drums and eager, bloodthirsty shouts echoed through the night and in the circle of the arena a row of torches lined the arena. Though a cool breeze moved through the city, Eohan felt too hot. *This might've been my fate. It might have been my brothers'.*

Trying to calm himself, he rubbed Cloudy's neck. They rode to a ditch filled with small corpses. Even in the darkness, Eohan could see the dirt stained with the color of iron.

Seweryn picked his way through the ditch. As expected, Eohan followed him.

Eohan stopped short as he saw in the grass nearby, a babe lay exposed. Her eyes open wide. Her ribs pressed through her discolored flesh; her neck was so thin each notch of her vertebrae was visible. Her tiny arms and legs twisted towards her distended stomach. Only the tri-pointed ears showed she was a Fairsinge.

"Eohan."

He didn't move. He was frozen.

Kajsa put her ear to the child's bare chest and listened. She closed the child's eyes. "We're too late. I'm

81

sorry."

"What happened to her?"

"The child's mother is probably in the arena somewhere. A servant, a fighter, concubine -- we can't know."

This is what Alana saved me from, Eohan thought. *I'll never doubt her again, no matter what the Guild says.*

"This should do."

"Good. We need to get the boys out of here," Kajsa said.

The word "boys" rang out in Eohan's ears. *I'm nineteen summers and acting in the manner of a boy!*

Seweryn grunted in the darkness as he and Doriel lifted a corpse of a light-skinned Daosithian boy approximately Kian's age.

Unable to hide the tremble in his arms, Eohan took the legs from Doriel. The kid was so thin, it looked as if he hadn't eaten for weeks before he died. He set the body on an oiled tarp. Doriel cut off the ears of another Fairsinge and slipped them into the tarp which Seweryn tied to the saddle of his horse.

✳

"**B**UT, MY LORD, HE DOESN'T LOOK LIKE me?" Kian said, peering at the corpse of the Daosithian boy which would be his replacement.

Seweryn's face flushed and his eyes flickered upwards.

"No, but he will. Seweryn's an artist," Kajsa said as she pulled out a deck of card from her pack. "Don't pester him."

Kian shoved down a whimper when Seweryn grasped his hair. "Not enough length in the roots," he said.

"How much do you need?" Kajsa asked. The cards clattered against each other.

"Only an inch from you and maybe an inch from Roark to add a bit of red."

Kajsa clipped an inch off her braided beard.

Roark frowned but allowed Doriel to clip off a few inch-long locks from the base of his neck.

With a small sharp blade, Seweryn sliced into the corpse's face and flayed the skin from the nose.

In the corner, Eohan rubbed his neck as he tried to focus on the card game with Roark, Kajsa, and Doriel, but Kian couldn't turn away.

Seweryn shaved a bit of cartilage off the point and used it to widen the frontal bone. With a bit of glue, he recovered the nose with flesh.

Seweryn shaved the eyebrows of the corpse and carefully replaced them with Kajsa's blond hair, in the edges he wove in a bit of Roark's auburn hair. He carefully shaped the brows to mimic Kian's. He wet the lashes with lemon juice. "Before you complain, I know the color won't be perfect, but how often do people study the lashes."

The corpse's head fell back as Seweryn lifted him and adjusted a basin.

He opened a jar of sour milk and mixed it with a thick oil then ran it through the dead boy's hair. The curls straightened. As he had with the brows, Seweryn wove in some auburn highlights into the boy's hair.

Kian shivered. He fought the compulsion to run his hands over the dead boy's face. "My lord, the resemblance is uncanny. Han, you got to look at this. Come look."

His brother did not rise from his spot on the table. His normally tanned complexion had taken on a distinct gray pallor.

Roark patted Eohan's forearm and called back, "I should think your brother prefers not to see you deceased."

Seweryn rolled the boy onto his stomach. Like Kian, the boy had scars on his back. Yet, he asked Kian to lift his tunic to match the major scars. He even matched the three moles on his shoulder.

Pressing his blade again the corpses scalp Seweryn cut off the dead boy's ears and sewed on the Fairsinge ears which Doriel procured for him.

"My lord, that is amazing."

"Not my best work, but it'll do for a corpse." Seweryn covered the body with the oiled tarp before he walked outside and pumped water to clean himself.

⚹

Chapter 10
The Great House of Josael
in the Realm of Daouail

KAJSA AND SEWERYN ROAD INTO JOSAEL. The path into the Daosith capital was coated in crushed white petals and lined with white, green and black bunting, most likely left over from the coronation celebrations.

From the road, the Empress's palace, with its spiraling towers and arcing domes looked peaceful, but Kajsa knew the Empress of Daouail would be guarded and might even have a truthsayer amongst her advisors. As long as the boys remained with Doriel, they would be safe, but she didn't like crossing into any elfkin city without her brother.

They were greeted politely, but there was mistrust from the guardsman to the stablehands to the herald who called out her noble name quickly and to the point, followed by Lord Seweryn and every relative he ever had.

Finally, they were led through the heavy wooden doors to the Great Hall.

The opulent carved white stone was filled with dancing light from the stained-glass windows. Fireplaces were set every ten paces or so, and between the fireplaces were groups of the elfkin generational portraits.

At the head of the hall sat the Empress upon her

throne. A woman of twenty-six, her obsidian skin glowed with youthful radiance the way many young elfkin do, but the opal and emerald crown sitting on her head threatened to crush her slender neck.

Kajsa bowed; Seweryn lay the oiled tarp on the floor and knelt. "Empress. It is my great honor to present, Lady Kajsa, Daughter of the House of Goldvein, and this of which you seek."

He opened the tarp. "We have found the boy Kian for you."

The Empress nodded, still balancing the crown upon her head, but her courtiers dove towards the body, screaming and hitting it with their hands while shouting, "We gave you a home!" and "We gave you a position!"

Kajsa was careful not to show emotion, but with the knowledge that it would be even easier to hide any discrepancies between Kian and this boy, she inwardly smiled.

"Enough!" the Empress said. "Tell me how did you come across this murderer?"

Feigning ignorance in the ways of the Daouail, Kajsa spoke in the language of her people while Seweryn translated. She specifically made mistakes in her diction, so Seweryn needed to ever so slightly, shift the meanings of her words. "On the peak of Laithmor, we found this child, beaten and stabbed. Between gasping breaths, the boy told us he was Kian, a runaway slave from the House of Josael. He cried, for his name would be one with a murderer, and cried for his mother who he hadn't seen in nearly two years."

Kajsa was interrupted by the grumbles of the court, but the Empress sat still, her piercing violet eyes never leaving her face.

"When Roson found him that night, Kian was only looking to get a sip of wine. Roson told him he would know freedom if Kian got him out of the castle.

The boy was innocent of your grandmother's murder. He didn't even know she was dead until they made it to a town where they met up with an acquaintance of Roson. If you investigate the body, you shall note Roson and his brutish friend treated him cruelly over the days; and when they were stopped in Daubmor, they stabbed him, then left him to die either from his wounds or exposure."

"If they were seen in Daubmor, were they from the Guild?" The Empress asked.

Kajsa worried this question would come up but answered smoothly: "Misunderstandings between the Guild and the ruling class frighten my people too. If there was a contract, it did not come from the Guild House on Laithmor."

The Empress nodded.

"Thus, in good faith, I rode to you in order to find the murderer and return the royal ruby to its place for the amount of the bounty."

"And if it's the Guild?"

Kajsa liked the straightforwardness of this Empress's questioning. "Empress, you will have your satisfaction. Is there anyone who can reasonably answer questions about these slaves?"

The Empress said to her herald. "Bring Cook to me."

The Daosith cook hurried into the Great Hall. He dropped to his knees in front of the Empress and pressed his face to the floor. However, Kajsa still detected the week-old purplish welt which graced his dark plump middle-aged face.

"Is this the boy, Kian?" The Empress asked.

Trembling, the cook side-eyed the body. "It looks like him, your Highness."

"Do you wish to face my interrogators?"

"No, no. I know how to be sure. His face is scratched. May I touch the body, your Highness?"

She gestured for him to continue.

The cook bent down and gingerly touching the corpse, he pulled down the boy's tunic and exposed the shoulder.

Yes, your Highness, yes. It is him."

"How do you know?"

"These moles on his shoulder; Kian had moles there."

When this wasn't challenged, the cook looked on his back. "Highness, his back bears the scars he received from Lord Josael, may the royal consort's spirit be resurrected on high."

This supplication made the entire court shift in discomfort, including the Empress. However, she sat straighter and looked older than her twenty-six years. Kajsa could see the Empress's thoughts as if the dancing light of the windows had formed images. The entire court remembered the affairs, gambling, misuse of slaves and servants. No matter what people thought of the wise, ancient Empress; her consort had been loved by none.

Seweryn raised his hand and spoke in the traditional manner. "Friend of mine, speak with an open heart, so we may we know the truth in the service of your Empress and in service to all the Realms. The Guild seeks the truth in this matter. Rise and speak. In front of these many witnesses, may no one raise a hand or voice for your memories or they will face the might of the Guild."

The Cook glanced at the Empress.

"Speak," the Empress said.

The cook shifted his weight and rose to his feet. His voice creaked, and he did not raise his eyes. "The boy was used to pay a debt ..." He gulped. "Kian came to my kitchen, frightened, but he knew how to cook."

"Any problems, anything at all, no matter how small the detail?" Seweryn asked.

"Well, he was a boy, and once or twice made a

boy's mistake. I'd give him a smack, and he'd not do it again."

"Such as?"

"He was supposed to be watching a pie, but it burnt. He apparently was taking sips from the dregs from a used carafe. I sobered him up with a good smack. He never did it again."

"Cook, I believe this boy to be innocent of the crimes of larceny and regicide, just a boy who perhaps woke up when the knife was stolen," the Empress said. "Tell us what you know about the other slave, Roson."

The cook shifted his weight on one foot, then the other. "But I don't know him. I never spoke to him. I only saw when they brought him in in chains through the butter door. That night, when I took to my pallet, Kian was already in his. In the morning, I realized Kian was gone. I informed the magistrate. They kept asking questions I can't know."

"Cook," the Empress said softly, "Return to your duties in peace. I thank you for your honesty -- even when there is painful truth to be heard." And as if to prove her point, the Empress stood and curtsied.

The cook's dark eyes teared. He bowed lower to the Empress and backed out and into the darkness of the servant's corridor. The entire court looked to be in awe too. The Empress may have never expected to rule, but she was a wise woman. Perhaps the Empress and Royal Consort's deaths would dawn a new day on House Josael, but thinking about the Cook's injuries, she doubted it.

❊

Chapter 11
The Guild House of Laithmor
in the Realm of Daouail

SIX DAYS WAITING, AND ANOTHER SIX TO wait. Roark hoped he'd made the right decision by hiring Kajsa and waiting at Laithmor.

Thunk. The dagger missed the target, which Doriel had set up for him in the Great Room of Kajsa's chamber. He hit the wooden beam beside it.

"Your arm's getting stronger," Eohan said.

Kian mumbled something and ran to get the knife. He threw it again.

Thunk. Kian's bare feet slapped the stone.

Roark thought about showing Kian to learn to walk softly, but he wasn't the master, and if he acted thus, they would never be friends. Maybe that's why Doriel didn't order them. With Kajsa not around, Doriel was more dour, more like Seweryn. Roark wondered how he didn't notice it before. Only in the prime hours when Doriel practiced with Roark and Eohan in a daily skirmish did he seem happy. He never gave any encouragement or discouragement. They just exercised. Then he ordered lunch. He never told the apprentices what to do. He didn't seem to care whether they were there or not. At night, he kissed the locket his wife bestowed upon him and laid on his bed, and the three apprentices returned to the rented cabinet each night to sleep in the sizable Guild bed. Though a small, plain room with the three of them, it was cozy enough.

Thunk. Kian hit the target. The knife bounced and clattered to the floor.

"Good show!" Eohan said.

Kian ran to retrieve it.

Roark thought about returning to the cabinet where he could have time alone but knew if he left the other two would follow. A pecking on the door grabbed his attention. A gull waddled in and squawked. Roark checked the scroll tube. "Alana sent us information," he said, excited for the distraction.

Alana had scrawled a quick note about where she had been -- including visits to Edar Candlewick followed by a longer description of the stone's true use and composition which he copied in code into his journal. As the letter went on, Alana explained that she didn't know the exact location for Daena, but suggested seeking a place within the principality, but a few days ride from the castle. Someplace quiet.

With a quick, "I need to run to the library, but I'll be back soon," Roark dashed out the door.

He ran silently down the hall, happy for the moments of freedom without the other boys. Briefly, he wondered if Alana felt this way about her apprentices. He dismissed the thought as he opened the heavy oaken door to the library.

Soft light flickered from oil lamps reflected by mirrors. Books and scrolls covered every horizontal surface. Some were digests on strategy while others were the personal journals of war enders, assassins, intelligent officers.

"How can I help you, Apprentice?" An old Daosith hobbled toward him on her cane.

"I need a map of Daouail, Librarian."

"Certainly, your master has such a thing."

"I mean a large one, something that shows details of landmasses and roads. It's for a lesson."

"Lady Alana is a comprehensive instructor."

Wondering how she knew Alana was his master, Roark chose the safest answer which happened to be the truth. "That she is, as is Lord Corwin."

The librarian glanced at the door, then leaned closer. "Pray, are they still an item? Many histories find my stacks, but very little gossip."

Still not having any idea who he was talking to, but trying to be polite, he said, "No, my lady, their daughter's death pains them still."

"Indeed, not surprising with those two's passions. Please give Alana my sympathies."

Ignoring the mention of his aunt's "passions," Roark replied, "I will, my lady."

"I'd offer the same to Corwin, but he'd not accept them. When they were both war ending, not all the armies of the Seven Realms could stand against them. Did you know their long romance was the subject of several songs?"

Roark must have looked uncomfortable, because the venerable librarian laughed and led Roark to a wall with a large spiraling family tree showing the Daosith, Fairsinge, and Fate Great Houses. "Did your cousin have any children?"

"No."

She wrote a symbol under Saray's name. "I was never able to ask Alana, her pain is so great. Let's get you a map."

The librarian unrolled a large map of Daouail on the centermost table and turned on lamps to illuminate it. Roark carefully studied Seweryn's province, Illuminual, until the librarian left. He focused on Josael and its environments. The Great House was located in the most clement and populated region of the highlands. However, the rivers flowed from the highlands into a large, flat alluvial plain in the southwest corner of the principality. A few farming hamlets were located to the east of the wide, meandering river, but the land on the other side was densely forested.

Roark copied it carefully into his journal. This had to be where Daena had gone. His plan was coming together.

※

Chapter 12
Province of Sildeir in the Realm of Fairdhel

THE THREE FAMILIAR SUNS OF FAIRDHEL danced overhead. Alana was glad to touch Fairdhel soil, but her mind was on the boys. Alana counted her charges once more. She and Byronia had found five children from her list and seven enslaved adults, four Fairsinge, and three Daosith.

Byronia rented a covered wagon in order to transport the children while the adults would walk beside it. The driver, Jaith, was a round man with a kind heart -- especially when Byronia offered to pay twice the usual rate to help keep an eye on the children. His daughter (and apprentice), Jana, had her father's good temperament. A cheerful girl of twelve, she drove the cart beside him. Yet she enjoyed scampering about with the rest of the children or gossiping with Balrea and Caraine while the elder girls played with Balrea's moppet. A driver knew the dangers of the road well enough that Jaith would be armed, and he would have at least a passing measure of ability. Still, she counted Jaith and Jana among her charges.

The freed citizens kept up a constant stream of chatter. If there was danger on the road, they would have to face it head on; there was no chance of stealth. Still, even at this slow pace, only four days travel between the port at Olentir and the capital city of Sildeir which bore the same name.

Dry branches rubbed together in the breeze. The wind whipped through the grasses. The first day, they passed Guild members, unsurprising since they were so close to the Guild House. As the suns set below the horizon, the party made camp at a known caravan site.

Focused on brushing Talia, Alana shivered under the moonless night. She knew she could not push the party faster, but each day at this slow pace was an eternity. *Damn Corwin and damn me for allowing myself to be indebted to him.* She told herself: *Roark and Eohan are both nearly grown; allow them to be men.*

They heard voices coming from the trees. On the edge of the dell, they saw four men armed with wooden cudgels. One also had a knife on his belt. They were dragging several women and children bound with ropes. Seeing the group, it was as Alana feared: There were Fairsinge slavers who cared not about enslaving their own.

"We can't run in time. Everyone who cannot fight, get into the wagon," Alana ordered.

Byronia looked frightened, but she drew her sword.

Jaith and Jana both drew long spears.

"Looks like four, milady," Jaith said.

Alana smiled. "I'd like to lure them in."

"As it pleases, milady," Jana said with a resolute nod. She might still be a slip of a girl, but at twelve, she had seen the road's violence.

Alana, Byronia, and Jaith hid in the nearby brush.

The four men laughed when they saw Jana alone, pretending to shoe her ox. One made a half-hearted swing of his cudgel, believing Jana was not going to be any trouble. She spun around and backed towards the tree where Alana hid.

Talia broke through the underbrush as Alana brandished her double blades. She could hear Byronia and Jaith charge. With her left hand, she stabbed the neck of the slaver grabbing the oxen. Clutching on the spurting wound, the man raised his club with his free hand and grabbed the at the girl. Jana spun again and knocked him back with her spear.

Jaith took the opponent closest to him, and Byronia slashed her saber at the man holding the bound slaves. By the screams, it sounded like the others were making progress, but Alana was too busy with her two opponents to check.

She thrust her left-hand dagger into her second opponent's shoulder, missing the neck. In response, the man made a wide fast swing of his cudgel and Talia reared up in order to miss the blow.

Alana pulled the dagger she kept in her boot and threw it without taking aim. It still landed true, slicing open the man's neck. He pushed his hand on the wound, but he was bleeding quickly. He swung his cudgel once more, this time the blow was weakened. Talia kicked him to the ground where his blood flowed freely. Alana wondered how that blood would taste. She missed Edar's potions and regretted not accepting his offer.

Ignoring that need, she turned to see if any of her allies needed assistance. Byronia's opponent was bleeding with mortal wounds, and she was freeing the women and children. Jaith was stomping the life out of his opponent.

After all, the man had tried to put his filthy hands on his daughter.

The adult citizens came out of the wagon and kneeled in front of them and sang their praises.

Once they began moving again, Byronia asked quietly, "Is it always like this?"

"The road?"

"The praise. It shames me to think my people have suffered under my negligence."

"Learn from your shame."

※

Village of Macotir

THROUGH THE THINNED TREES ALONG THE river, Alana spotted a billow of smoke showing the location of the village of Macotir.

As they drew closer, they could hear working. Axes chopping wood. A plow breaking ground, and the swears of a farmer pulling up roots. Above it, all was the constant ping of the blacksmith's hammer moving metal.

"Look, someone's there!" One of the men's voices called neared the wagon, his words choked with tears.

A hastily-built stone wall surrounded several huts which bore scorched scars. Three old men sat in front of the gate.

"Who goes there?" One asked, holding his ax high in the air.

"Don't be a fool. Are you blind? Look, it's Balrea and Balhan and Caraine!" One cried.

"How did you escape?"

The three elderly men crowded around the wagon. The sound of work stopped in the village and men and women rushed forward.

Caraine called out for her mother, but her voice was drowned by questions and embracing arms.

Alana caught a look of panic on the child's face as she tried to back away from the grasping hands and kissing mouths. Her shoulder's sagged; Alana grabbed her before she collapsed.

"Eohan!" A large man roared as he hurried towards the gate. Tears streaming down his face. "Eohan! Has my son returned?"

Keeping Caraine under her arm, Alana put her hand out. "No, but I bring word if you would call him your son, Gouren Smith. Where is Fol Baker? I have news that concerns him as well."

Smith's eyes opened wide, his cheeks flushed, and he stepped back. "You are the Martlet of House Sildeir?"

Though she wasn't entirely sympathetic with a man who denied his son's existence, she felt a twinge of Eohan's bitterness. "No, that would be Lady Byronia younder. I am Lady Alana of House Eyreid, I asked: where is Fol Baker?"

Smith winced and wrung his hands. "Fol is not here. He went to beg for help at the Great House. I ought to have gone with him. Every night I am haunted. Milady, please, what word do you have of my son, his mother, and brother?" So the man had realized his foolishness.

"To ease your heart," Alana said. "Aedell died on the slave ship, but Eohan brought honor to his mother's memory by helping us rescue all the surviving women and children. Though born a butcher, his deeds are worthy of a nobleborn. I'm proud to call him my apprentice. He and Kian are with my nephew Roark."

Tears swam in Smith's eyes.

"Caraine is ill." Alana said, "We need rest, our horses need to be fed and watered if you please."

"Come, I have little, but it's yours."

Alana followed the smith to his shop. Grime over the bellows. Cobwebs lined the corners, but the shared heat from the forge kept it warm.

"Take a seat, milady. Caraine, if you need rest, you can sleep there." He gestured towards a large hay pallet on the far side of the room.

"Now we're away from everyone, I'm better," the girl said, still hanging onto Alana's hand.

"Well, your color is still pale," Alana said. "If you

don't wish to rest, sit quietly."

Caraine cuddled beside Alana on the bench. Eventually, she laid under her arm and rested her head on her lap.

Smith quickly chopped more carrots and threw them in his throws his pottage which bubbled on the fire.

"You're kind to her," he said. He did not say for a nobleborn, but Alana heard it in his rebuking tone.

"I learned her mother is the Wisewoman Ylsabet."

"Aye."

"And she is in Eyredeir."

"I used to have a young boy, name of Iav around, but he was carried off, too."

"If he survived, Byronia and I will find him. We seek the children who were sold before Roark, and I could save them."

Smith pressed his lips together. "Caraine was ... sold ... that's why you've been gone so long. And why she looks sickly, while some of the others are strong ..." Smith paused, "Milady, what do you apprentice my boy in? As a commoner, it's not like he can be a Martlet."

"I'm apprenticing both of Aedell's sons in War Ending. I am also a Guild War Ender as House Eyreid is not so large that its Martlets don't need a job to pay the bills."

Smith's eyes darted around. "In truth, milady? You wander?"

"For the good of our people," Alana answered.

"Why haven't we ever seen you or any other Martlet?"

"Because in any generation there are only fourteen active Fairsinge Martlets and thirteen Daosith Martlets. In order to help those in need, we chase the ruin. I came because ruin came to your village and Lady Byronia needed my help to find who was lost."

"If you find Iav. Tell him I am alive, and he was a

good apprentice, and he can come here to me if he wishes ... Or, by your word as a noblewoman, will you find him a good apprenticeship if he wishes to stay there?"

"By my word, if he is alive, he will have a vocation -- and he will not live as a slave."

"Good." Smith looked down at his massive hands. "I know I wasn't a father to Eohan. Even when he wanted me to be. When you see him again, you tell him, that I am sorry."

Alana said she would. But it was too late. Eohan would never be Gouren Smith's son.

※

Elizabeth Guizzetti

Chapter 13
The Great House of Silba
in the Realm of Fairhdel

WITH ONLY CARAINE, THE CARAVAN MADE better time as it wove up the mountain road towards Sildeir. The twelve round towers of House Silba, one of the oldest great houses in Fairdhel, dominated the skyline. As the party continued up the hill, Alana could make out the amber-colored granite stone walls which connected each tower. Thin, arched windows are scattered across the walls in a seemingly random pattern, along with overhanging battlements for archers. Though this stronghold had been once made for conflict, it was softened by centuries of ivy and climbing flowers which scaled the walls. Below, the walled village was protected by a massive portcullis and sharp-eyed soldiers. Sildeir was a larger city than Eyredeir and the good roads between it and the Guild house at Olentir and the port city of Dundir. Sildeir's mines brought out some of the purest ore in the Seven Realms. Though the city was named for silver, there were also nearby mines containing copper and iron. Carts, boxes, tents and various trade goods were stacked and packed outside the village walls, ready to be sold.

They passed through the heavy iron gate where

the sentries gave them wide smiles and bowed at Byronia and Alana.

A boy was sent with a message to the Great House. Inside the walls, stablekeepers hurried to take the horses. The gardens were alive with red and gold blossoms. Byronia scanned the garden, but she kept smoothing her travel clothing and adjusting her scabbards. "We should go in immediately." She bit her lip. "If you think that's right."

"Orla is your sister. I'll follow your lead."

The carved wooden doors of the inner keep opened into the Great Hall. Stepping past the stone statues which supported the great loadstone. The first generation of House Silba had been carved in stone, but, past the statues, the Great Hall was set up in the standard Fairsinge way. Alana was transported to the time in which she and Corwin visited House Silba together to announce her pregnancy and discuss in which House the child would be named. So many years ago, but very little had changed except the latest generation of freshly painted portraits.

At the head of the hall sat Doyenne Orla upon her throne and her husband sat beside her. Alana had known she had at least one child, but the girl was young, still in the nursery. Lady Falka wore the simple robes of a priestess as was her station. The fourth born, Aldran, smiled at them in a way that made it hard to read what he was thinking. He was a fair young man. Hopefully, he would make a loyal husband someday. Perhaps due to Corwin's urging a match had been made already.

Orla stood in her heavy blue velvets that matched her deep blue eyes. "Lady Alana of House Eyreid, I bid you welcome, and thank you for your service to our people. Sister, I am gladdened you have returned."

Byronia curtsied at her sister. Alana did not as she had no need to. Caraine knelt.

"It was my pleasure, but I need to get back to my apprentices," Alana said.

"Wait," Orla called. "We must ask more of you ..."

Alana already could see what the Doyenne was thinking. More rescues. The Doyenne motioned her herald, who scurried from the room.

He returned with a lanky man that resembled Kian who practically swept the floor with his bows.

"Fol Baker made a petition when his wife and sons were stolen."

"I have news." Alana quickly filled the hall with the story about how she had found Eohan alive on a slave ship, how Aedell had already died, and how she sought for his young brother and found him. (She did not speak of Kian's shames or the Regicide and assumed she would not be asked as Orla obviously had other things on her mind.)

"Our citizens have taken refuge in Eyredeir, but there is no need when they might return home," Orla said. "And then this child might be reunited with her mother."

"Send an ambassador to my sister with an escort for the citizenry's safe journey of. I protect our people; I don't tell them where to live," Alana said.

"I have. There has been no answer. We could hold you until we receive one," Orla said.

Byronia's eyes opened wider. The older lady did not believe the younger had led her into a trap and ultimately it didn't matter. *Orla was Doyenne and young people are often so stupidly headstrong in how they see the world.*

"I don't believe that you would make threats against an ancient ally," Alana said.

"I'm not threatening you, but we must have our citizens returned to us. They are important to Sildeir."

"Not important enough for you to fight slavers,

just important enough for you to fight your allies."

"Wait ..."

Alana turned to go and looked down at the girl still on her knees.

As she suspected, she was quickly arrested and taken to a guest room. Four mice squeaked when the door opened, and they ran in all directions, seeking to crawl through a hole in the wall.

So the slavers -- or something -- are draining House Silba's wealth. No wonder Orla would gamble so much to save those lost. No wonder Orla ordered her sister to wander.

She asked her guard, "Since I'm here at the Doyenne's convenience, might I be bathed, and my clothes laundered?"

As she suspected, her needs were promptly met.

❋

ONCE NIGHT FELL, ALANA SLIPPED FROM her window and climbed the tower with the hope that the House was generally maintained, the way it had been when she and Corwin were lovers.

She reached the roof, slid through a tight opening, and climbed upon a joist. Rodents scurried past her, their tiny claws clattering on the attic floorboards. She crossed the timber without fail. She scrambled down the other side of the tower and entered the Great Hall's roof space the same way. Below, servants were cleaning, their children were playing with a large, brown spotted atair whose floppy ears bounced as it's six legs padded around them. Atairs always faithful pets and patient guardians of children, the animal glanced roofwards a few times and howled. Alana held her breath, but no one bothered to look up. She quickly crossed the joists to the kitchen.

Staying close to the wall, she silently slipped

through the corridor and down the stairs to the visiting commoner's quarters: a large room filled with pallets.

Alana crept in the darkness careful not to make too much noise until she saw the familiar frame of poor Caraine slumped on her pallet weeping into her hands.

Alana kneeled before her. "Don't cry. I'm taking you to your mother."

The girl's voice was too loud as she sobbed. "But the Doyenne said ...."

Alana thought a curse but did not speak it in front of the girl.

The baker coughed behind her and whispered, "If you're taking Caraine to her mother, would you take me to my sons? I heard of your battles. I've never fought, but I'll keep an eye on the girl and make myself useful. I'm a good cook."

Caraine started shivering. "But Baker what if ... they find us ..."

"Did anyone lay a hand on this child?"

"I'm not telling you, lest they lose it. But I haven't -- and won't -- lay a hand on her. I don't blame her for what happened. I blame them," he hissed and gathered the girl into her blankets. "Now, listen to milady."

Caraine took Alana's hand.

No one stopped them as they left the common visitor's hall to the Chapel of the Thirteen. They crossed the garden to the stable, where a sleepy stableboy prepared Talia. She hoped he would be smart enough in the morning to not be chastised.

Escaping was easier than it should have been. That worried her, but there was nothing to be done about it. Behind her, Caraine leaned into her back and began to softly snore. Before the girl fell, Alana tied a spare cloak around her. Fol Baker jogged beside. Good to his word, he kept up with Talia as best as he could without complaint until they crossed the plain to the seaport, Dundir.

As the suns rose into the sky, Alana found no Guild ships but saw a long grain ship. An errand boy ran to and fro, and the captain, a Fairsinge woman, stood beside a painted sign that read PASSAGES AND MESSAGES TO SANDIER, MARDIER, EYREDEIR AVAILABLE. The crew, both Daosithian and Fairsinge, wore thin, threadbare tunics and trousers that looked like they hadn't been washed in a fortnight. As they approached, though the crew looked thin, the ship was in good condition.

"Let's see about that one," Alana said.

The symmetrical shaped-hull were protected by wales and featured wing-like projections and a large housing to shelter the rudder system. Between the starboard and port posts were the folded glass hull for InterRealm travel, but other than a small cabin situated at the stern with a place for the steersman, the decking was exposed to the three suns.

"Excuse me, Captain; do you have any passage below deck? And stables for my horse?" Alana asked.

She licked her flaking lips. "I keep a single fine cabin and stables, but it'd be fifty sovereigns."

"I'll pay forty now, and if my horse is in good health when we arrive, you will get an additional twenty."

"Let me see the money."

Alana showed the captain the money along with her Martlet broach. The captain grunted and called, "Gavon."

A too-skinny boy of nine raced down the gangplank. His bare feet slapping against the weathered wood.

They were led past men hauling bags of grain up the wide gangplank.

As they crossed the deck, Alana witnessed too-slender parents giving crusts of bread to their too-slender children. Their eyes followed her as they followed Gavon through the hatch.

"Stay close to me, I wouldn't half-surprised if we were robbed."

"If the Martlets really wandered, the elfkin wouldn't suffer," Fol muttered.

Talia was stabled in a dirty looking stable beside a brace of birds and a drift of hogs. She snorted, obviously unhappy.

Gavon led them to a small, dank room. It's only separation from the rest of the ship was a red curtain. Other than the chamberpot in the corner, its only asset was they would remain below deck.

"The captain will be having a laugh with his purser," Alana said looking around at the bare room.

Gavon returned carrying three hammocks.

A youngish woman, who resembled Gavon, followed with a musty log book. Her loose tunic threatened to fall off her narrow shoulders as she bowed. "Cap said, forty now, twenty ashore?"

Alana inclined her head at her and handed her the forty.

She plopped onto the deck and counted it slowly while Gavon quickly ran the hammock ropes around her. Once satisfied, the purser wrote Roark out a receipt. "Many thanks, milady, ..."

"Alana, the thirty-seventh Martlet of House Eyreid."

"I suppose you'll be wanting all the comfort this ship will give?"

Gavon opened his mouth wide and tugged at her wrist.

Alana took a step back. "Purser, I, my friends and I only wish for transport." She took a package of smoked rabbit and handed it to her. "Eat here, so it isn't taken from you."

The purser took the meat, sat down on the deck

and tore it into two uneven halves. As Alana expected she would, she gave Gavon the bigger piece, before devouring hers in seconds.

Orders echoed through the ship. The purser grabbed the ship's log and purse in one hand and Gavon by the other. They raced out. Once the sailors were out of earshot, Alana smiled at the others. "Perhaps some lanolin would be in order?"

"That'd be good." Fol nodded.

A commotion was heard above them. Hoofbeats. She heard Gavon, but no other. Byronia. Still, there was nothing to be done. She tucked Caraine into a hammock furthest from the door. Fol sat below the hammock and held the girl's hand.

Byronia entered the room, her hands in clear view. "You might have told me we were leaving; I almost missed our transport."

Alana made no move for her weaponry as Gavon brought in another hammock and strung it up. Once the boy was gone, she said, "I'm returning this child to her mother."

"We know. Orla said you were a very bad example. So I said, 'Orla, you told me to be a Martlet. A Martlet wanders for the good of our people. Alana just wants to reunite these families.' And took my leave."

"With permission?"

Byronia's deep blue eyes, which mirrored the Fairsinge sea outside the porthole, held wretchedness. "Orla knows I went after you, but I need not permission to fulfill my vows." Still, the young Martlet walked over to Caraine's hammock. "You've suffered enough for several lifetimes. By my life or death, I shall find your mother and bring you to her. You and she can see to your future; it is not mine to dictate. I wander for the good of my people."

A white gull screeched as it waddled down the

stairs. It shuffled to Byronia who took the message.

"Uncle says: Keep to Alana's lessons. I'm a Martlet now, no longer a child pretending to be one. I guess Orla complained to him, too."

"The court rarely understand us, yet you and your sister have long been friends, you shouldn't worry." Alana tossed the gull a bit of bread, who caught it and flapped up to Caraine. It nestled into the blankets with her.

"I'm not," Byronia lied, her eyes set on the grungy hammock where she would sleep. Alana handed her the lanolin.

❋

Elizabeth Guizzetti

Chapter 14
Province of Josael
in the Realm of Daouail

GROUNDWATER SEEPED OVER KIAN'S leather shoes; icy brackish water squished between his toes as he followed Eohan, trying to stay in his brother's footsteps.

He lifted his head just in time to see Cloudy stumble.

She jerked forward, knocking Eohan back as she sank into the muck. His brother jumped out of range of her frantic steps and scurried around in front of her. Eohan tightened the bridle and calmed her with soothing words. She cried a heart-wrenching scream.

Jaci and the other horses whinnied in reply.

Cloudy's leg lifted; it was coated with blood.

The party moved to higher ground. Kajsa quickly pulled out bandages.

"Best we leave the horses here. Kian, can you be trusted with caring for the animals?" Kajsa asked. "Perhaps even brush some of this mud off?"

"Yes, my lady. May I have a fire?"

Kajsa looked around. "See that hillock? Let's put you on the lee with the horses. They can graze."

The party progressed towards the higher ground.

Kajsa found an acceptable spot and lit him a fire. Doriel set up a cooking pot and threw tubers. The blaze seemed insignificant against the water and the scrawny bare trees whose twisting branches reached for a way out of the infernal damp mist.

Roark and Eohan took short lengths of leather from the saddlebags and tied the front right leg to the back leg of each horse while speaking gentle words of comfort. Seweryn unwrapped a bundle of hay and spread it around the hillock. "Keep your eyes on the horses. They'll most likely try to stay on the firmer ground of the hill and only go to the water to drink. Just remember they're stronger than you if startled."

"Yes, my lord."

Kian watched the others sink into the muck as they moved in a southwesterly direction. He wished for the familiar comfort of wine.

Alone, Kian drew his knees to his chest and forced the sobs to remain in his chest. Insects alighted on Kian's skin, but the scent of Seweryn's potion forced them to fly before they bit. Hating the idea he was useless, he pulled out a brush from Seweryn's saddle bag. Kian curried each horse as well as he was able.

He changed into dry clothing and put on Eohan's short riding cloak. He sat with his back to the fire, his eyes on the hobbled horses.

Kian wiped a tear from his eye. For the months he was enslaved, he couldn't remember Ma, it hurt him too much. Now he couldn't not see her singing.

Chop, Chop, Chop the pork,
Grind, Grind, Grind the pork....

He could see Pa coming in with the day's leftover buns and breadcrumbs. They would kiss, and Pa would give the boys a treat.

"Don't spoil your supper," he'd say.

He wiped another tear away. He took a sip of

water and recapped the water skin. It wasn't wine, but at least he didn't hurt anymore.

The swamp's quiet was broken by a splash, but when he turned around the water's surface was flat. "Just a fish or an eel ..." He shivered. In the distance, something broke the surface, but he couldn't identify it—or even if he really saw anything. "Calm down, you're acting like a kid."

Jaci whinnied, her eyes wide. He rubbed her snout.

Out of the corner of his eye, he spotted blackness crest the water again. This time closer. Ochre was near the water's edge!

Not knowing the words to get the horse to move, but hoping his meaning was clear, he shouted, "Ochre, back! Here, girl!"

He grabbed a stick from the ground, raced across the hillock just as a sleek black mass crested the waves, its huge maw open wide.

Ochre lifted her head away from the beast's snapping teeth and shuffled backward up the hill as well as she could in her hobble strap.

Kian smashed the stick across the large furry back. The wood split, useless. Kian threw the piece still in his hand. It struck on the side of its head. He grabbed another large stick. With a haunting screech, the beast disappeared into the water.

With a rope, Kian created a corral for the horses to keep them away from the dark water. He took one of Seweryn's oiled tarps and dipped it into the water and tied it between the small threes hoping to make some sort of trough. The trees creaked as they bent inward but held.

With the hope the party would return soon, he collected as many stout sticks that he could without touching the water.

Chapter 15
Province of Eryedeir in the Realm of Fairhdel

DISEMBARKING THE SHIP, ALANA BREATHED in the air of home. The smell of the sea. The call of gulls and eagles as they soared on the wind. The gleaming six white towers growing out of the granite cliffs -- the westernmost one held her comfortable apartment -- though she rarely stayed there.

They moved down the long wooden docks, commoners bowed and tried to kiss their hands, their horses. As they reached the shore, more commoners surrounded them.

Behind Alana, Caraine cried, "Mama!" and slid to the ground.

The girl tried to push her way through the crowd but was pressed back by the mass of people.

"Caraine!" the wisewoman cried. "My child."

"Byronia, if you please."

Byronia dismounted and shouted, "Move aside by order of the Martlet of House Silba."

Everyone stopped moving, including Ylsabet. As if she strode into battle with all the confidence of a hardened warrior, Byronia took the girl's hand and led her to the wisewoman who had sunk to her knees. The woman stretched out but remained in place.

Tears streamed down the woman's face. She kissed Byronia's hands. Confidence faltering, the Lady of House Silba tried to back away.

"One of my lost children has been returned." Ylsabet kissed Caraine's cheeks and pressed her to her chest and rocked her. "Caraine! You found her as you claimed you would, Lady Alana. Lady of House Silba."

Alana touched the woman's shoulder. "Your daughter has three more mornings and nights of medicine. Lady Byronia and I must go to the Great House. Can you keep Fol Baker until I return his sons to him?"

❄

WHISPERS OF THEIR ARRIVAL FLEW towards the castle. The party slowly made their way through town and continued up the limestone road, which spiraled over the curvature of the hillside until they came to three arching oak and iron gates. The sentries gave them wide smiles.

Inside the walls, the garden was ablaze with vivid red and yellow flowers of the season. Stablekeepers hurried to take the horses.

"Let's speak to Laraena and Ylynn."

"Do you think your sister will return the hospitality my sister gave you?"

"Probably not. She's not fool enough to believe she could hold a Martlet. We should write to Corwin. If Roark could use our help, we should go, if not, we'll wait."

"You're willing to wait?"

"Corwin's right. It's time for Roark to be tested and we might get better descriptions from the parents when it's time to find the others to help you in your continued travels."

Byronia smiled softly.

"What is it?"

"Corwin won't believe you said he was right."

❉

Elizabeth Guizzetti

Chapter 16
Province of Josael
in the Realm of Daouail

EOHAN COULDN'T TELL WHICH SMELLED worse, the rotting swamp or their bodies. Though the air was cool and the water frigid, a sheen of sweat covered each of their foreheads and dripped from their noses and chins as they slowly moved through the muck. They crawled over and under the slimy bark and twisted, exposed roots. Their woolens were soon covered in brackish water and mud. Turtles lazily swam away from their movements. Eohan's boots grew heavy with mud, his pants and tunic were coated with it. What he wouldn't give for a fresh stream.

Kajsa slid into the muck. It burped as it swallowed her.

"Ka—!" Doriel cried. By the time his voice hit the second syllable, Kajsa swam back to the surface, her tunic sparkling with blood.

"Tree hollow. Careful," she said.

Ignoring her warning, Seweryn splashed over to her. He lifted her tunic and rinsed her wound with fresh water and covered it with a bandage. He took another step, sliced himself on the same hidden tree root.

Seweryn rinsed and bound his calf as well as he

could on one leg. A shrieking howl echoed all around them. It sounded from the east to the west. In front and behind.

They tried to move to higher ground, but the swamp halted their progress. The howl sounded again, and this time it seemed right to be behind the nearest tree.

A sleek furry beast, at least seventeen hands, leapt out of the water and landed on Roark, pulling him under. Eohan reached for his friend but missed before he disappeared from view.

The beast crested again. Roark was still alive, splashing and gulping for air.

Kajsa, Doriel, and Seweryn all had their knives in hand and flung them before Eohan could even see. The beast screamed as at least one hit its mark. It dove again, and Eohan chased until he found Roark on his knees coughing and choking up mud. Though he wanted to go after the creature, he helped his friend to his feet and brought him back to the party. He saw one bloody knife in the mud. He picked it up, unsure whose it was.

Doriel saw it. "I missed eh?"

"There's blood on it, but it didn't stick."

"I should've practiced with Kian then," Doriel replied.

While Seweryn looked over Roark, Kajsa suggested opening the map again, but they couldn't find the suns behind the mists. She opened her Realm compass -- a gift from Alana -- to discover the direction.

Yet it mattered little. The mists were so thick there was no time. He had no idea how far Kian and the horses were from him. How long the boy had been left alone. Time was elusive in the mists.

He fell into the hole which captured Kajsa and Seweryn.

Staggering out, Eohan yelled, "We're moving in

circles."

"Or the swamp's changing," Doriel said and held out a hand to him.

"This place is maddening." Eohan felt the tremble in his arms as he tried to scrape the muck from his clothing. He clenched his fists.

Suddenly Kajsa had his muddy shirt front. She pulled him to his knees so she could look him in the eye.

"I might not be your master, but you listen good: a War Ender can never lose their temper," Kajsa said. "Alana's right, you have it in you, but you lose your temper, and you might as well go home and be a butcher or baker or whatever in the lowest Realm that you did before this." She flicked his ear for good measure then turned around, trying to find some light in the trees.

Heat rose to Eohan's cheeks as Roark came up beside him. "Thanks for saving me. We ought to tell Alana that her vision was correct."

Eohan swallowed his fury and shivered, this time from the cold wetness all around him. Once his anger faded, he thought: *A War Ender examines all assets.* "I have an idea! Roark, have you ever been able to read minds with those you can't see? Maybe you could sense her presence?"

Roark's brows knitted together. "I've never tried it, but I'll try." He closed his eyes. His corpse fell back into the water. Eohan hauled him out. He was dead weight. His neck and arms flopped backward. "He's not breathing!"

Seweryn pressed Roark's neck with his fingers. He ripped open the muddy tunic and listened to his heart.

"Shit, Alana will kill us all," Doriel said.

"Come back, come back, Roark." Kajsa took his limp hand in hers.

As quickly as the life left him, it returned. Roark gasped out. "Oh, sard, no. Not like we thought." He started coughing, tried to stand and vomited into the water. "No. Sarding." He gulped in air and clasped onto Seweryn as he was closest. "I went away. But I found her. I'll never take my body for granted again."

"Where is she?" Kajsa asked.

"Not far, To the east." Roark pointed, outspread his hands trembled. "She doesn't know we're here. Lots of spells though. Fairy fire. I saw Kian. He's been collecting wood. Got a good pile of sticks."

"He's a good boy," Kajsa pulled out her journal. "There's a common enough counterspell for fairy fire."

In the seconds that followed, chaos again impeded the party.

Two swamp hags, wet black braids whipping wildly, brown mud covering their darker flesh, lunged at Roark and howled. Another two rose to the surface of the muck grabbed Eohan, and another two grabbed Seweryn.

"Don't look into their eyes!" Roark screamed.

"What brings you to our domain, guild lords?"

Eohan took a step back from the ancient Daosithian women but found his feet were stuck in the thick mud.

Kajsa barreled into their midst without heed of their long black claws with two arms out, each holding a short blade. One hit squarely, and blood sprayed into the dark water. The second was a glancing blow, but that was more than enough to drive the second hag away.

"Move," she shouted.

"I can't!" Eohan was sinking. They were all sinking. The water rose to his knees, to his thighs, the cold burned up his waist. Kajsa and Doriel disappeared under water. Roark was up to his chin, gasping for air. Eohan reached for the branch above him. It broke way in his hands. He thrashed.

Kajsa gripped Eohan's forearm. He was where he had been.

Another howl echoed through the swamp as Doriel brought down his battleax on the shoulder of the hag who held Roark. He hit another square in the ribcage. He followed Kajsa to Seweryn who had one on his back and fighting off another. "Mother forgive me ... I don't want to be a War Ender," Seweryn muttered as if in a daze, staring at a reflection in the water.

Kajsa knocked the one off his back. Seweryn shook his head and drew his sword. A turn and he sliced through the middle of the swamp hag in front of him. The bodies sank into the muck and water.

Eohan could not see them, but he could barely see his feet. "Will Kian be alright?"

"I think Roark's astral projection brought her. As long as Kian doesn't use any of the mystic's tools, he should be safe." Seweryn said.

"Her? But there were six," Eohan said. "And where did they go!"

"No, there was one. Always only one and even she is just a shade set to make us turn back," Seweryn said. "That's why there was six and not ten. She didn't sense the dwarves at all. Just us three."

The party moved forward until they came to a flashing white light. Roark approached it first; it grew larger and hotter until he backed away.

Seweryn raised his hands at the level of the flame and carefully spoke the most common counterspell for fairy fire.

The wind lifted, and the air became icy, but the fairy fire remained constant.

Seweryn sliced open his forearm. He flicked blood on the flames and spoke the magic words. The wind grew even wilder; still, the white flames sparkled and burned.

"This is not the right way."

"But your blood gave me an idea," Doriel said. He wet his cloak into the muck and held it away from his body. As he drew closer, the flames grew. He dropped his cloak onto the flames.

For a moment it sputtered.

"Now!" Doriel shouted.

Eohan dashed through the opening. Then the fire grew sparked and grew. It swallowed Doriel but opened up a gap.

"Go, Go!" the dwarf screamed, trying to smother the fire with wet mud. Roark passed in the gap.

"Go, go. I'll help Doriel," Seweryn screamed. "Go, go. Kajsa go."

Kajsa followed them. Seweryn smothered the flames on his arm. The flames rose again, cutting them off from their two companions.

"This better be worth it, or I'll kill you both," Kajsa growled at them.

※

KIAN LIFTED HIS HEAD TOWARDS THE splashing of water and grumbling. It sounded like Doriel, but he couldn't be sure. The silhouettes of two people -- a lanky elf and a stout dwarf broke through the mists.

Towards them, he saw the outline of black fur break the water's surface.

"Look out! There's a monster in the water," Kian screamed.

The sleek creature moved quicker this time as it set its course towards the two men who seemed to be moving in slow motion. Grabbing another large stick, Kian jumped into the water and barreled towards them. "My lords! There's something in the water!" he screamed again.

Seweryn's saber flashed in the dim light as he left Doriel leaning against a tree. The elf disappeared somewhere in the mists.

The black furry mass dove back below the surface and veered towards the dwarf.

With speed Kian didn't expect, Doriel leapt, his braids flying about his face and a deadly-looking knife in his right hand.

The beast bounded out of the water towards him, and the dwarf plunged a knife into its head. The beast howled a cry worthy of a banshee, fell back, shaking its head trying to dislodge the blade. Seweryn stabbed it, drew back his sword, and stabbed it again.

It howled and sank below the surface.

Doriel leaned down and pulled out his knife which he wiped on the hem of his muddy tunic.

"See, my friend, nothing to worry about. I still have my right hand." Doriel kept his voice jovial, his skin was the color of flour paste and coated in perspiration. "Are you alright, lad?"

"I kept it away from the horses, my lords. I wouldn't let it hurt them."

"Good lad."

"Help me with Doriel; he's more injured than he'll let on," Seweryn said.

"Really, don't make a fuss," he said, rocking and holding his left arm to his chest.

Kian hurried to the other side of Doriel and put his arm around his waist. He was amazed at the weight of the dwarf who began wheezing.

Doriel collapsed on the wet ground near the fire.

Seweryn ripped open the sleeve on the injured arm. Pustules sparkled with dried crystals, glittering like granite. Seweryn pressed his fingers against the inner wrist, the flesh didn't move with the pressure. "Oh Goddesses, no pulse. Do you feel that at all?"

"No."

"Try to move your fingers."

"Gods, I can't. I've petrified."

"I'll have to amputate."

Doriel closed his eyes and stroked his long beard. "It's good it's my left hand. I'll lose my battle ax, but not my sword hand." He opened his eyes again. "Do it with my ax."

Listening to the men's' argument, Kian fought the urge to vomit.

Seweryn dug in his saddlebag for a bottle which he handed to Doriel who gulped the contents quickly and set it on the ground.

With the sudden urge to know what mysteries Seweryn knew, Kian pressed Doriel's arm. The flesh was hard as stone. The petrification ran from Doriel's fingertips to halfway to Doriel's elbow. "Isn't there another way?"

"Not in this swamp. Take the fist, Kian. Hold it tight."

Kian grabbed the petrified hand. Seweryn marked a line with ink in the still movable flesh. Doriel whispered a prayer to a mountain god, each word slurring a bit more than the last.

Seweryn drew Doriel's ax into the air and brought it down against the arm on the mark which he made. Doriel screamed. The scream echoed off the water again and again. The horses nickered, unhappy with the sound. Blood spurted upwards.

Seweryn packed the wound with an iron-colored powder.

Kian wanted to cry. Doriel took his stone arm from him, looked at it and tossed it off the hillock and into the mud. "Elfkin magic won't ever kill a dwarf."

"Why in the lowest Realm did you take the risk?" Seweryn asked.

"I didn't think the flame would swallow me like that."

"What can I do for you?" Kian asked.

"Pshaw," Doriel said. "You're a mother hen just like Seweryn. Just need a stout ale to make me right."

"The best I can do is a Daosithian wine," Seweryn said.

"That'll do."

Looking at the first discarded bottle sitting in the wet ground, Kian noticed a small amount on the bottom. *How sweet the wine would be.* He only wanted the dregs. *No, I don't!* He screamed in his head. *I want to go home. I want to hear my mother sing and one of Pa's stories. No wine. No blood. I must be Kian again.*

❋

ROARK SLIPPED TOWARDS THE SMALL STONE house built on the dry hillock. It was quiet except for the light movements inside. Even in the dim of the swamp, herbs grew in the windowsills. With his back against the wall, he used a mirror to see inside. Daena was sitting at a table, eating what looked to be porridge and reading a scroll. She looked to be a Daosith woman of four decades, her long black locks were set in a thick braid, except for the scowl on her face. According to Alana, she was twice that age. Who knew what else they would find inside? Roark wished he could talk to her. He wished to know what she knew. And he knew this would be denied. He crept towards the rear of the cottage to the fire wall where Kajsa and Eohan waited.

"Sometimes the Guild should be seen," Kajsa said. "Eohan. Go in through the windows in the back. I want her to feel surrounded. Roark, on me."

Kajsa climbed the hillock and examined the front door. "Don't see a trap but that didn't mean one doesn't exist."

She pushed it open and jumped back. The hinges

whined. A moment later, a flash of fire scattered over the front stone stoop. It hissed as it landed on the wet, muddy ground. Kajsa leapt over the fire and rolled into the door. Roark jumped in behind her.

"How dare you!" A woman's voice yelled. Daena scrambled towards her pantry and grabbed a large crock. She threw it towards Kajsa who knocked it out of the air. The crock fell to the ground and shattered.

Holding a silk rope, Kajsa snapped her arms wide as she leapt at Daena. They tumbled towards the floor. Daena screamed. Keeping her muscles tight, Kajsa rolled to her feet and dragging Daena to her knees. She pulled the rope taut, but not tight enough to strangle. Still, the woman's fingers pressed against the rope out of instinct, scratching her own throat.

Eohan clambered through the back windows. He looked most impressive with his claymore drawn, though it was impractical for indoor use. The boys advanced upon the necromancer though Kajsa has her well in hand.

Roark realized, *This is no opponent. She's just a woman hiding in a swamp.*

"Stop fighting, I don't want to hurt you," Kajsa said. "We want to return the ruby to your cousin, so she might rule in wisdom."

"She sent the Guild?"

"She posted for a reward for the ruby's return, and your cousin pays well enough for my apprentices and me to be interested," Kajsa said.

Daena hung her head. "It doesn't work. It's nothing to her—or you."

"Can you pay what she does?"

Daena opened her mouth.

"What do I care if it works? All I care about is the bag of gold I'll receive once I return the bounty."

"And what do I receive?"

"We'll leave you in peace with a bit of advice. I'd

not return to court if I were you. Two runaway slaves were first suspected of your cousin's death and killed in your place, but I questioned the Empress about the stone. She may suspect."

Roark stopped listening to Kajsa and read the scroll on the table. It was only a friendly missive to a swamp hag, inviting her to dinner. His stomach plummeted. He hoped Seweryn was right and the Swamp Hags which attacked were only shades of the original.

I thought I was just killing the Empress and her consort, but regicides hurt so many more. As long as I'm part of the Guild, I can never be clean. In his mind, he recited: *The Guild keeps the Realms safe for free and peaceful trade. The Guild keeps the Realms safe for free and peaceful trade. The Guild keeps the Realms safe for free and peaceful trade.*

✳

Elizabeth Guizzetti

Chapter 17
Guild House of Olentir
in the Realm of Fairdhel

EOHAN DID NOT LIKE HOW KIAN STARED AT the House Master or possibly the ruby as the old man carefully removed the quartz from the setting. Corwin measured the stone and examined it for flaws. He dug through a bin of unpolished rubies until he found a large, clean piece of rough, close to an inch long and wide.

Eohan reached for his brother as he stepped closer. The House Master did not even bother to look up as he polished the gemstone with a rough awl. Slivers of red stone slid on a piece of felt. Rubies, even slivers of rubies, would buy so many things. Eohan learned to master his greed by one of Alana's not-so-gentle lessons. He never wanted Kian to be disarmed, knocked from his horse and left for several hours alone in a dark wood to think about what he had done. He did not doubt any lesson from Corwin would be much worse.

"It's very much what Lord Seweryn did with the bodies, isn't it?" Kian asked.

"Indeed, lad, it is." In a soft voice, he began to explain how he was grinding the shape close into that of the finished stone. He stopped and carefully examined the gem. "I must identify any flaws, and remove them, except this one, which matches the one in the Empress's ruby."

Roark looked at Eohan. "Who in lowest Realm is this?"

"Kian doesn't annoy me nearly as much as you two do," Corwin said and pressed the gem into a grinding wheel until a flat surface appeared. "This is the face of the stone, and I'll use this flat to orient the rest of it as I grind in the facets. Fetch that pot of wax for me."

Kian ran to get it and brought it back.

Eohan shrugged at Roark. And met his eyes. He hoped Roark would read his mind. *Probably best Kian doesn't know the House Master as we know him.*

Roark nodded.

Corwin attached the flat of the preformed gem to a flat-faced brass dop stick with a big dollop of black wax. "First, I grind the lower portion which is called a cullet into shape ..." He rechecked the Empress's stone until the shape matched. He removed the stone from the first dop, carefully attached it to another dop, and ground the crown of the gem into shape.

After Corwin had cut and polished all the facets, he removed the sparkling gem from the dop. He softened the wax over a candle and removed most of the wax. He dropped the gem into a jar of whiskey.

❈

WATCHING KAJSA AND SEWERYN RIDE toward the docks, Roark hoped the trickery would work. That he wasn't sending his friends to their deaths. He hoped the Empress would like the ruby.

Now he was injured, what would happen to Doriel if Kajsa fell? His wife was dead; he had no House of his own.

"Doriel will be fine. Plenty of Guildmembers have amputations," Corwin said, coming up the stairs behind Roark. "I've been watching your mind, and I'd remind you the future demands we hold back technology. Remember the schism when you doubt the wisdom."

"But Lord Corwin, if you read my journal or Alana's, you'd see what the species are doing to each other and themselves. If you ever left your Guild House, if you saw the bodies of children at the arena ..." Roark's voice got caught as he choked with emotion.

"My patience with your and Alana's nonsense grows thin."

Roark decided to try another tact. "My lord, you want to rule this Guild House with wisdom. You claim you plan to study the gem ..."

"Careful how your tongue waggles," Corwin said. "I could throw you from this tower, and only Alana would care. Come, if you are truly to be a journeyman of the Guild, it's time to show you something."

Corwin cast a light sphere and placed it above his head. Roark followed the House Master to the rear of his chamber coated in darkness. He could hear the swishing of the linen against the stone floor and see the outline of the silvery hair and robes move through a doorway, but he couldn't see the floor beneath his feet. The air felt cooler with each step. Roark ran his hand against the stone wall and felt for the stone stairs as he slowly and silently moved through a corridor that was previously unknown to him.

Darkness washed over him, and he felt his knees weaken.

"Alana thinks I am foolish to only want the nobility as the elfkin representatives within the Guild," Corwin said getting further in front of him. "But I will show you what I have seen, and perhaps you will understand why I am against anyone who has greed and ambition in their hearts."

"But Eohan ..." Roark stopped the words on his tongue. He knew Eohan was ambitious.

"Good, you're learning. I've taken no pleasure in trying to force some sense into that soft brain of yours. I have told Alana many times that she is too gentle with her apprentices."

"Yes, House Master." Roark felt for another step, still unsure of Corwin's goals for this tete-a-tete.

"Alana is correct. Eohan is a steadfast friend to you, but he sees himself reaching a station above which he was born," Corwin said. "If you ignore what is in front of your eyes, you will fall."

"Yes, House Master, but Kian moderates that." It was the best thing Roark could think to say in the moment which was truth and protective of his friends' characters.

"Correct. Eohan's drive to be a good brother -- and a good man -- is greater than his greed."

"Why don't you want him in the Guild?"

"If I didn't want him in the Guild, he would be dead." Corwin spoke with such simplicity and straightforwardness, Roark saw the truth in the words.

At the bottom of the stairs, the light sphere rose to the ceiling illuminating a cavernous chamber filled dozens of wheeled carts and carriages bursting with circuity, and metal bits lay unused and covered in dust. Paint peeled off metal exposing rust. "Are these vehicles, House Master?"

"These used to be the engines of the Realms that polluted the water and air. But that is not what I wanted to show you."

They went deeper into the graveyard and through a gated archway. Corwin cast another light globe which went towards the ceiling illuminating a large black tube which seemed to swallow the light around it. Below it lay a few bodies, untouched by time.

Roark took a step back. Corwin gestured him to follow.

"We no longer know it's true name. This is the weapon that caused the last schism," Corwin said. "Guild scholars know it is powered by the Realm's gravitational pull. The last Monarch gave it to the Guild for safekeeping and as a symbol of trust and unity. She feared letting it the fall into the wrong hands. All intelligent societies keep making the same mistakes, including ours. Until society stops grasping for power, wealth, even for personal gain, the Guild must hold technology back. Even history cannot tell us which of the Monarch's children was to be the most just leader before the schism. Only that one compensated scientists to build weapons that shattered our Realms."

"My travels taught me that humans, dwarves, and gnomes all had such weapons," Roark said. "All intelligent species claim to cause the schism."

"Perhaps we all did." With a deep sigh, Corwin leaned upon a thick wooden beam and held out the blood quartz which shimmered in the flickering light of the sphere. "If I take this quartz and try to use it, am I any better than the nobility which claimed this weapon -- and others like it -- were only used for good?"

"But wisdom isn't the same as political power."

"Greed is an insidious thing, and it is known to topple the wise. Did not the Empress, whom you murdered, allow her consort to take pleasure in slaves?"

The young man pinched his eyes shut, stopping the words which formed in his heart.

"Speak."

The young man feared Corwin would strike him or leave him in the darkness with the other corpses, but he had been ordered to speak. "But, my lord, if we fear everything, we can't better society either. Alana says the post Schism ways are fading. Something will take its place whether the Guild wants it to or not."

Corwin sighed again. "If your life hadn't been spared when my daughter fell, I might've loved you as Alana does." He pressed a hand to Roark's chest.

Roark's exact thoughts developed into words which bubbled up his throat and escaped his mouth. "House Master, the necromancers have apothecary knowledge the Guild doesn't have. It wasn't swords that killed Saray, but the wounds. I sat beside her deathbed and held her hand as she gasped her last breath. It bubbled and stank with infection."

The old man smiled. "This is why you have my leave to study necromancy. Edar Candlewick's death won't come from my hands but anticipate it if too many learn your secrets. I'll expect reports every cycle of Dynion's moon. Tell me not only of your successes, but your failures as well."

Corwin took Roark's hand set the quartz inside. "Keep it hidden. It's supposed to be in the Guild Vault." He called back the light sphere and walked back towards the stairs. "I will write my congratulations to your parents. They shall be gladdened to know their son has become Lord Roark in the eyes of their ally."

※

Chapter 18
Province of Eryedeir in the Realm of Fairhdel

R IDING BEHIND EOHAN IN THE NIGHT, KIAN couldn't see anyone on the streets, though in the distance he caught a glimpse of the six white towers growing out of the granite cliffs above the sea. Several barges were moored at the docks. Below the towers, a small village surrounded by a stone wall, which looked as if it was carved out of the granite cliffs.

The songs of nightbirds, the gruff voices of nightguards keeping the peace and shepherds caring for their flocks, echoed off the shoreline.

As they passed the first village gate, the nightguard bowed at Roark. A young boy or girl, Kian couldn't see clearly in the dim light, dashed out of the gatehouse to let the stablemaster know that Roark approached. "Her Highness and your great sister prepared a mighty feast for you, Master Roark. Your mother's eyes shine bright with pride for you."

Kian wished his mother's eyes still shined.

Inside cottages and pubs, a few villagers shuffled about, but the streets were quiet other than the clops of Cloudy and Jaci's hooves on the limestone street. Kian felt trepidation and joy as the Great House grew larger as the road spiraled up the hillside.

Inside the walls, firelight danced along the path. Even in darkness, the garden was bright with color. Stablekeepers hurried to take the horses. As they dismounted. Alana ran out to greet them, her long silver hair caught by the wind. Though her braids blew around her, without armor and dirty traveling clothes, she looked less like a wild witch now, more like someone's grandmother.

She embraced all three boys. Kian glanced at the older boys. Eohan was blushing with embarrassment but looked pleased. Roark looked comfortable in his aunt's embrace and accepted her kiss on his brow.

"Though it pained me to stay out of the way, I knew you could accomplish this feat," she said. Her voice held a mixture of pride and sadness. She turned to Eohan and Kian. "Welcome to Eryedeir. So Kian, what did you think of your first adventure?"

"I'm not sure, Lady Alana."

"Well, my apartment has been made ready for your arrival. You'll get cleaned up, then pay your respects to the Doyenne. In the morning, you can see your father."

Eohan smiled: "You found him?"

Kian's heart felt light and fluttery. "Pa's here?"

"Yes. And in Eyredeir, yes," Alana answered both questions. "He has been watching the road for days, but the hour is late, and since you didn't see him, we must assume he is asleep. Though I have much respect for your dear father, Roark's mother is the Doyenne, and you must pay your respects to her."

Kian nodded, though he had no real understanding of such things. What he knew was he must obey Lady Alana the way Eohan did. Obedience was his shield. He didn't know what might happen to him in the Great House.

They passed the inner guards when the high stone walls closed in on him. He gasped unable to get in a full breath. Lady Alana was beside him, holding him up. She pricked her finger and put a drop of blood on his tongue. "No one may cause you any pain within these walls. No one, do you understand?"

"Yes, my lady." His heart slowed by the memory of blood. He felt stronger.

＊

F RESH GRAVEL CRUNCHED UNDERFOOT AS they passed the newly constructed buildings for the refuges. Eohan walked in pace with Roark and Alana to the wisewoman's house. A sluggish pain pulsed above his eye, Kian kept him awake for most of the night with new terrors and pacing. He wanted to see Pa but felt a strange sorrow and fear he could not name. To calm himself, he tried to analyze his surroundings, as Alana had taught. Now she was back, it was easier to remember her many lessons.

The two-story apartments were built quickly but looked to be of better construction than the old butchery in his own village.

Kian hurried in front of them. "Come on!"

"Go ahead," Alana said with sadness on her face.

Eohan wished to question her, but he couldn't. He feared the moment he opened his mouth he might weep. At the end of the street, Kian dashed into the apothecary shop with a sign with a silhouette of a woman in the family way and the words "Wisewoman Available" in the window.

Kian's feet resonated off the wooden steps, and he shouted, "Pa!"

"Your pa's upstairs," the wisewoman said when they entered.

Caraine, one of Kian's old playmates, was behind the counter, watching them. Ice coated Eohan's heart as he met her eyes. He thought of the brothels he'd seen, the arena, the beautiful but terrible Great House which held Kian. A lump formed in his throat and his heart beat faster. Ignoring the fear quickly morphing into panic, he returned to analysis. *I'm alive. Kian's alive. Pa's alive. We're all free. What's wrong?*

The smell of fresh pitch and cut timber overwhelmed him as he squeezed his way up the narrow stairs. He heard Pa cry, "Ki!"

He found Kian in Pa's arms. They both wept.

Eohan wiped his eyes with his sleeve.

With one arm around Kian, Pa wrapped his other arm around Eohan's shoulder. He returned his embrace, even slouching to make it easier for Pa, who at the time Eohan was stolen was still a finger width taller than he. Now Pa was nearly a hand shorter. He accepted the kisses on his brow and cheeks. Pa felt bony under his thin, stained woolen tunic. His shoe leather had been patched multiple times with numerous pieces of thick thread.

He glanced at Alana and Roark who sat together on a narrow bench, their eyes on the scene in front of them but providing them distance. He wondered what Roark thought. Roark's father was elegant and while aloof, genial enough to Eohan the last time he visited. *Lady Alana was alone with Pa for several days; what does she think?*

"I feared I'd never see you again, Han," Pa choked.

Any learned War Ender's analysis failed. His nose grew full of snot. A surge of tears burned his eyes before they slid down his cheek. "I thought you were dead -- I told myself you were dead. It's like you've come back to life."

"Lady Alana told me how you rescued your brother. I'm so proud of you, Han." Pa said, his voice scratched and reedy. Tears tumbled down his face.

"Just look at you both. Growing like weeds."

Through tears, Pa made observations of the both of them, told them of the kindness of Lady Alana and Lady Byronia of House Silba.

At the words, House Silba, Eohan's mind sensed a threat and automatically fell into analyzing Pa's words.

"I can't wait to take you home and get back to normal life," Pa said.

There it is. Life in a tiny village of a hundred felt suffocating, claustrophobic. Eohan straightened and stepped enough.

The direction *"speak your mind"* flashed in his awareness. Unsure if it was Alana's thought or his own, he cleared his throat and wiped his face with his sleeve. "Pa, I don't have words for how much I missed you, Ma, and Kian till I found him. But I'm not returning home. I plan to stay with Lady Alana. I am a bound apprentice of the Guild."

Pa's brow furrowed. "I don't believe ..." His shoulders slumped forward, and he gripped Kian tighter. "No ... I raised you. You don't have the cold heart of a noble-born ... warrior." Every word grew more unintelligible until Pa sobbed.

Kian's cheeks grew scarlet with fury; his eyes red from crying. "Who are you to act like, a lord?"

"I'm simply Eohan, but my eyes have seen much."

"... Tempted by the wealth," Pa cried.

Eohan knew he was tempted by the finer things, but that wasn't it. He didn't want to leave his friends, and the idea of never seeing Nalla again slashed his heart in two. "I like the work. It's bloody, but I save people!"

"You can never be a Martlet; you're just the son of a butcher and baker," Kian shouted. "Just like me!"

Between sobs, Pa formed the words. "Lady Alana, tell my son, he can come home. My boys know all Aedell's recipes. Together they'd have the finest shop. They can pay you back!"

"Eohan and Kian owe me nothing. Cloudy will find a home in Larenna's stables," Alana said from the bench. "Go with your father if that is what is in your heart. And Smith regrets not knowing you."

Eohan clenched his fists. His nails pressed into his palms. "But I'm bound to the Guild."

"You're an apprentice who worked with a handful of agents. No one will request you once you are gone. Your birds will grow old in their roosts and after a few generations be bound to another," Alana said. "You still can walk away from this life."

"These fancy tunics don't make us lords, Han." Kian hissed, nearly spitting.

"One day, your noble friends will rip it off your back," Pa said.

Alana pinched her lips together but said nothing.

"They will put you in a barrel and roll you down a hill," Pa cried. "Make you dance on coals."

"Then so be it."

"Auntie, tell them what you saw," Roark said. "Make them understand I'd never do that to them. You'd never do that."

"The vision tells much, and nothing. They either trust us or don't." She rested her hand in his.

Kian kept shouting. "Even if they don't betray you, you still might be eaten by a monster, so don't tell us what Lady Alana *thinks* she knows. You can't know. Neither can she; neither can Roark."

"I know that if I hadn't gone with Lady Alana that night, you'd be nothing more than a beaten slave under the thumb of a vic--"

Pa slapped him. "My son wouldn't speak to his brother like that."

Eohan raised his hand to his cheek though the slap hadn't hurt, the words were needles piercing his heart. *A War Ender never loses their temper.* He smothered all emotions and sat beside Roark. Angry crescents purpled his hands, but the flesh of his palm wasn't ripped. Roark put his hand on his shoulder and squeezed. He had never been so grateful for his friend's presence.

Alana put herself between the bench and Pa and Kian. "Enough shouting. All of you. Kian, Eohan is my apprentice. If you'd like to learn the same skills, you can come. Or you are also free to go with your father."

"I can't go with you." Kian's expression changed. The angry blush on his cheeks faded as his chin dropped to his chest.

"Speak what's truly on your mind, or hold your tongue," Alana said.

Kian pinched his eyes shut. "I want to forget all this happened."

Eohan felt another needle in his heart.

"No matter where you go, you are Kian."

"You weren't there! I was scared when the swamp monster attacked. I don't belong with your kind," Kian said.

"But you fought them off and protected the horses," Roark said.

"Doriel was joking when Seweryn cut off his hand! Joking!"

"Everyone's scared in battle. I was scared ... Eohan was scared, even Doriel, Kajsa, and Seweryn fear battle."

"Please, milord, why must you tempt my sons?" To Kian and Eohan, Pa begged, "Come home. Just come home."

"I can't." Eohan sensed with those words, nothing would ever be the same with Pa again. "But I'll send money when I can."

"I need not filthy money," Pa said.

"For Kian then ..." Eohan said.

"Very well, we've taken up the wisewoman's

home long enough," Alana said. "Say goodbye, Eohan, then come along. Sooner would be better. The longer we linger, the more pain we cause." She went downstairs. Roark left behind her.

❋

EOHAN'S HEART ACHED AT THE PARTING, BUT he caught up with Roark and Alana as they walked to the Great House. They spoke in the old Pre-schism language, knowing most of the commoners lingering on the street and kneeling before them did not know it.

"But, my lady, your visions saw us all together as men," he stated in the same tongue, though he stumbled as he translated his thoughts into words and his diction wasn't clean.

"Many years stand between that future and today."

"So Kian will eventually come to the Guild?"

"Perhaps, or perhaps I misinterpreted what I saw. Lowest Realm, maybe your brother does become a butcher, and you were just on holiday."

"You don't believe that," Roark said.

"No. After Roark's feast, we will be following your father and Kian home, Eohan."

"Do you still think he thinks of me as his son?" Eohan asked.

"Fol's disappointed to be sure, but no good man stops loving his son because the son enters a vocation different from the one he wanted."

"But I'm not his son."

"Stupidity doesn't become a War Ender," Alana said in her *don't be a cumberworld* tone.

Eohan didn't wince away from the acid in her voice this time -- even in a foreign tongue, her meaning was clear. He felt lighter.

She turned to Roark. "I'll miss you terribly. What's your plan after your promotion?"

"Learn whatever I can from Edar."

"Send him my best, Byronia, and I found him to be a good informant. That may save him in the end. But keep your eyes open and trust few with his secrets."

"Corwin warned me of the same."

"I'll need an assassin sooner or later, how long would you like me to wait until I hire you?"

※

Chapter 19
The Great House Eyreid in the Realm of Fairhdel

"**A** BEAUTY SUCH AS YOURSELF, SHOULDN'T be afraid to smile, Master Roark," the artist complained.

Roark smiled as he stared out his window as the artist sketched his face from different angles. From his apartment, he could observe his mother's town down to the bay where ships carried the province's agricultural goods to other Fairsinge Countries and beyond the Expanse. Smaller personal ships of the Province's noble born neighbors also docked. He heard the merchants, smiths, and stablehands scurry about preparing for the feast, but he and Eohan sat in silence and watched the eagles soar between the cliffs. Occasionally, the birds turned close enough, and he could see the individual feathers moving in the breeze. He had believed Alana's vision, but Kian had not wanted to follow the path. Now he would be leaving Eohan for at least a few years.

There was a knock on the door, and without waiting, his father entered his apartment. "Are you finished?"

"Milord, what do you think of these?" The artist bowed and held out the parchment.

His father said, "A smile isn't very lordly. This one seems best."

"As you wish, milord." The artist said, his voice held a hint of disappointment.

Father threw an irritated glance at Eohan. "Why aren't you with your master?"

"I asked him to remain with me until I ride," Roark said.

"Is he one of your various lovers?"

Roark sensed the murmur of the artist, servants, and guards and felt their slight shifting while they were waiting to see what would happen.

He refused to be baited. "No, my Lord Father, we're just friends."

"Your mother and I will miss you. Your aunt has brought great glory to our House though she has also caused complications. I hope you will do better. We cannot really afford another Martlet like Alana."

"If you want your son's glory, I would suspect that you should expect complications, my Lord," Eohan said quietly.

His father didn't bother to answer, but Roark smiled at Eohan.

"Listen good, both of you. All the money she spent on saving these people is now lost to the House. We welcomed these refugees into our land, now Orla wants them back. We're in no position to say no. Some won't go willingly." The words came with such resentment behind it, Roark wished for his father to show his decency and gallantry in front of Eohan.

Alana entered, her mostly silver hair with a touch of auburn swinging freely for court.

She glanced at the artist's parchments. "Well done, Master Artist. You have captured my nephew's joyful countenance perfectly."

By his father's unnatural expression, Roark realized the depth of his father's dislike for his aunt. He tried to remember even one time that his father looked at him the way Fol Baker looked at his two sons.

"Milord said it won't do for his noble portrait," the artist said.

"I'll buy the sketch for my apartment then. Meet me later, and we'll discuss the price."

"Very good, milady."

Alana looked stronger with the layers of full court dress covering her slender limbs: deep blue velvet justacorps worn to the knee embroidered with the heraldry of House Eyreid covering an equal length deep blue vest and breeches underneath. Though it was fitted throughout her chest, the flared skirt, through the addition of gores and pleats, was loose enough to hide her weaponry. Though two rows of pearl buttons and buttonholes lined the length of the opening, the coat remained unfastened. It was old-fashioned and fussy compared to the slim-waist tunics Roark preferred to wear, but he was still excited for his Lordship and the clothing which proclaimed it.

His aunt kissed his cheek and took his arm. They followed his father into the Great Hall. What seemed like a thousand cheering voices rose as flower petals were tossed from the balconies. It snowed the colorful petals, fluttering as they landed onto the floor. They released their sweet perfume as they were crushed underfoot. The colored glass reflected upon the falling petals and noble audience's faces.

Between the fireplaces were groups of portraits hung by generation. The oldest restored many times, the previous few generations brighter. In Roark's generation, only three portraits hung upon the wall. His elder siblings and his cousin, Saray, looked down upon them. Their youthful, fresh faces each painted upon the earning of their title. Once his own portrait was finished, Roark would join them.

His knees trembled, he couldn't remember the

last time he saw the Great Hall so full. Nearly every Great House had someone in attendance. At the head of the hall sat his mother upon her throne and his family surrounded her. Roark's heart soared as she looked upon him with a smile alighting blue eyes that matched his own. Her long, silver curls spilled down her back. She stood tall in her perfect blue velvet gown. His father removed Roark's apprentice doublet from his shoulders, left his side and stepped beside her.

"This young man has his master's leave to wander."

Her husband was smiling with his mouth, but not his eyes. Roark's youngest brother, now out of the nursery, looked bored. His elder brother stood on the right at the house priests section, frowning. Roark's heart grew colder. Eohan and Kian truly loved each other. These people did not love him. His mother did, his sister did— probably. Alana did.

Alana said, "Sister, I return your blood in order for him to take the vow of a Martlet."

"Is it true you are ready to take the vow?" Laraena asked.

Roark fell to his knees. "Yes, my Lady Mother. I vow to wander, subsist on luck, and bring wealth into House Eyreid as Lady Alana did before me."

Tears crept up into his older sister's eyes as Ylynn took an engraved silver saber with a gold pommel and came forward. "You vow to use this sword in the service of our House and people?"

"Yes, I will." Roark kissed the sword.

"Let this weapon protect you."

She held the saber to Roark who took it and sheathed it. Even for the few moments, it lay in his hand, he felt its perfect balance. He would miss the silver saber he used as an apprentice, but one day it would go to his niece or nephew as it had gone to him. His sister rested an embossed and crested velvet knee-length coat upon his shoulders.

She kissed his cheeks. Then she was handed his Martlet's justacorps which she laid upon his shoulders.

The entire great room cheered again. A flood of movement surrounded him. Food began flowing from the kitchen.

His sister took him by the hand and led him to the head table. She gave him a quick hug and whispered, "I found my promotion strangely overwhelming." Sitting beside his parents, people chatted their congratulation. Faces swam in front of his eyes until Byronia made her way to him, her blonde hair sparkled in the dancing light.

"After your feast, I will be traveling back to Dynion to find the missing children," Byronia said. "Would you like to travel with me?"

Roark didn't normally go after women, but he felt connected to Byronia is some way. It wasn't lust, but something deeper than friendship. Roark felt his future in Byronia's hands. Perhaps it was because she was a Martlet. Perhaps it was because like him she disappointed her family.

"More errands for your uncle?" he asked.

"Perhaps."

"Is Edar safe?"

"I'd think that's up to you more than I."

"What do you know?"

"Only what's important -- and the rest I do not need to know."

Realizing he did not have to ask his aunt, he knew his apprenticeship was over. His childhood was over.

※

Elizabeth Guizzetti

Chapter 20
A forest in Fairhdel

THE PALE CRESCENT LINGERING IN THE SKY cut an icy light through the gloom of the forest. Kian wrapped his thick woolen cloak around him, wondering how his father fared in his thinner clothing. The silence was as suffocating as the cold darkness, but he didn't know what to say.

"Winter should be early this year," Pa said as he pushed leaves into a small pile, exposing the hard dirt below. He struck a flint. A speck of light and warmth grew until their campfire exposed the bare branches above them. Kian unpacked two tubers from the pack and stuck them in the fire, sending a few sparks skyward. Remembering his childhood, Kian asked, "Perhaps, you might tell me a story while we wait for them to cook?"

"A wandering myth has taken my elder son. You went on an adventure with Larcians, a Daosith, and became friends with a young lord, what stories could I tell?"

"I could tell ..."

"Ki, enough."

Kian tried to think of something to tell him. "Lord Roark taught me to quick draw a dagger; want to see?"

"If you wish," Pa said in a low monotone.

Kian removed the dagger from his scabbard so smoothly and quick he doubted his father even saw it, then spun around and threw a dagger at a nearby tree. The thunk as it entered the bark was satisfying.

Grinning, he looked at Pa, who scowled until he met Kian's eyes. Only then did Pa smile and nod.

"Well done."

"Do you think so?"

"Yes," Pa said without any pleasure in his voice.

"I can do it blindfolded too."

"Excellent," Pa said in the same monotone.

Kian retrieved the dagger, heart sinking. As his hand touched the cool metal, he knew he made a mistake. "What do you think Eohan's doing?" Kian asked, no longer caring if he angered his father.

"Probably learning many new things with the great lady," Pa replied, his voice caustic.

"Roark ..."

"You'll soon outgrow that fancy tunic, but don't you forget you're a baker's son." Pa gripped Kian by the arm and with his free hand, he shook his finger in the boy's face. "You consider him a friend, but his friendship is only pity. And Han, a Guild Master."

Hot anger flared in Kian's heart. "You don't even know Roark! And Han will always be my brother. That's what he said when we parted."

"He meant it, but he won't look back often."

Kian bit the inside of his cheek until he tasted his blood. The blood reminded him of the old hunger which he shoved down to his stomach. "He won't ever throw us aside. Don't you understand what he did for me! What Lady Alana did? What it cost her?"

"If he doesn't die in battle, maybe he will send some money home now and again. Maybe it will be enough to find you a partner in the merchant class, and maybe I won't die when I can't knead bread."

Kian hated that he was shouting at his pa but couldn't stop. "Is that all you see? That I'll need my brother to save me -- us -- from poverty?"

"What else is there to see?"

"He won't be saving me from poverty. I'll save myself."

Pa's grip tightened on his arm.

"Let me go." Kian clenched his eyes shut. He wasn't afraid of Pa -- not after what he had been through, but the furious urge to open his father's thin throat and leave him gasping terrified him.

Alana's face was calm as she removed Pa's hand from Kian's arm.

"You followed, my lady?" Kian asked.

"Did you not call me a witch in your mind?"

"You don't need to be mock us, milady," Pa said.

"I would never mock you. I ask your sons to look into the future and take the path that they desire." Alana put a finger on Kian's chin, forcing him to meet blue eyes so common in House Eyreid. He thought of Roark -- the epitome of a nobleman.

"Do you want the future of which your father speaks?" She asked.

"No. I don't know. I know I don't want Eohan to make me a marriage or send us money as if we were poor relations. I saw many things at the Guild: intelligence officers, surgeons, librarians … I've been thinking about all that since we parted."

"If you don't know your path; you belong with me," Pa said.

"Kian is near the same age as Roark when he started his apprenticeship. You can wander with me until we discover it, then the door can open for you."

"If you live outside your province, you'll dance on coals for sure."

"Pa." Kian rolled his eyes. He had met three

Martlets -- four if he counted Roark. None of them seemed interested in making him dance on coals.

"Promise me you'll never put them in a barrel full of spikes and roll them down a hill." Pa was serious.

"I've never put anyone in a barrel full of spikes and rolled them down a hill. I certainly wouldn't to my apprentices. If you don't want to be parted from your sons, I could find you a position at the Guild House at Olentir. The House Master and I have long been acquainted. Or perhaps in my sister's house. Otherwise, I'll bring you home. The boys will visit in Midwinter."

"How would the Guild treat a baker's sons?"

"The Guild has a long tradition of egalitarian education. House Master Corwin is a better man than he lets on."

"You know him well?"

"He's the 51st Martlet of House Silba. We moved through the ranks together until he sought his current position."

"If that's true, why aren't you a House Master?"

"I've no interest in or talent for administration," Alana said.

※

Chapter 21
Province of Josael in the Realm of Daouail

B YRONIA CREPT TOWARDS DAENA'S COTTAGE
following the directions, map, and the slave
Telchine. She felt slight remorse as sie lifted
branches or helped her over and under the twisting
muddy roots with always a polite: "Let me help you,
milady."

By their law, Telchine only enslaved their
criminals, but this young individual seemed too young
to be a criminal to be sold to someone who took hir
away from hir homeland to Dynion and sold hir on the
slaveblocks of Port Dentwort. Hir hair was too green,
hir eyes too bright and no cracks had formed in hir clay-
colored skin.

*I'm finally being taught what the Guild really is.
I need to learn if I can accept this. What had this young
person done to be worthy to be sold into slavery, then
sold to my uncle who gave him to me to kill?*

With every sweet word from the Telchine's mouth,
Byronia wished to retreat. Alana's lessons whispered in
her mind, but they did not overtake ten years of lessons
with her uncle. With every step in the muck, she pondered
over her vow until she came to the conclusion: *I wander
for the good of my people, and this Telchine is not of*

mine. Sie is a slave and criminal.

The two reached Daena's fairy fire. Byronia did not hesitate to cut hir throat and shoved hir into the flames from behind. The slaves gurgled, choking upon the clay spilling from hir throat as sie landed in the flames.

The Telchine's body spasmed as Byronia stepped on hir back to cross the dancing fairy flames which licked at her feet.

Byronia watched the dead body crumble back to the clay from which the Telchine was formed. "I hope your next life is better than this one," Byronia whispered. "May the Waters of Resurrection wash you clean."

Refusing to welcome the festering guilt, she silently ascended the muddy hill to a shuttered hut. With a gloved hand, Byronia silently extracted a dead frog from her belt pouch. She opened its skin and cut out its liver. She put the rest of the frog back in her pouch then protecting the liver.

This would be an interesting experience. She might not be in a family line, but at least she's a noble woman. A noble woman who dabbled in illegal technology.

Byronia left from the shadows and faced her mark. She shoved the frog's liver into her mouth.

Daena could not shout for help as her throat closed around her words. She scratched at her quickly-swelling mouth and throat.

Byronia checked for a pulse from the artery in her neck. Daena was still. She studied her dead eyes. She took her blade and opened her chest. The metal slid through into her flesh. Byronia cut out Daena's heart ensuring she left enough of the ventricles for Corwin's use and wrapped it in a tarred sack.

She searched the shelves until she located the crumbling moldy tome written by Thysta Candlewick and a newer volume written by Daena. Since she was alone, Byronia also searched for jewels, silks and anything else that she and her sisters might find enjoy or to fatten the family coffers. If Corwin was right and war was coming, then House Silba would need every advantage. She enjoyed her sisters' company too much to wish them death or any ill will for their fortune. She was third born, so she was a Martlet. It was an aging system of chance, sometimes it was best to play the hand she was dealt until something better came along.

※

ACKNOWLEDGMENTS

I am fortunate for the ability to pursue my passions--even when the first drafts don't turn out. The Martlet Series started out life as my second novel. Though I always loved the characters, I knew the original work had issues. Thankfully after being published a few times, I was able to look at the original novel with a more discerning eye. I realized the problem and broke the original manuscript up into novella sized chunks. Like *The War Ender's Apprentice*, *The Morality of the Necromancer* wasn't even in the original text. It was written literally because my first readers wondered what happened to Kian between the first novella and what's now the third novella, *The Assassin's Twisted Path*.

First of all, I would like to thank my darling husband for always believing in me.

I would also like to thank my editor, Joe Dacy II.

I would like to thank my writing group for believing in the project and to thank my friends at Two Hour Transport, since I started reading this novel aloud before it was edited.

I would also like to thank my fans who support my endeavors. Without you, none of this would be possible.

ABOUT THE AUTHOR

Much to her chagrin, Elizabeth Guizzetti discovered she was not a cyborg and growing up to be an otter would be impractical, so she began writing stories. Guizzetti currently lives in Seattle with her husband and two dogs. When not writing, she loves hiking and birdwatching.

Guizzetti loves to write science fiction, horror, and fantasy with social commentary mixed in – even when she doesn't mean it to be there. She is the author and illustrator of independent comics. She became a published author in 2012 and her debut novel, *Other Systems*, was a Finalist for the 2015 Canopus Award.

ALSO BY ELIZABETH GUIZZETTI

Comics published by ZB Publications

Faminelands
Out For Souls&Cookies!
Lure

Fantasy published by ZB Publications

The Grove

Science Fiction published by 48Fourteen

Other Systems
The Light Side of the Moon

www.ingramcontent.com/pod-product-compliance
Lightning Source LLC
Chambersburg PA
CBHW021046130626
46552CB00005B/2042